By the same author

The Princess Stakes Murder

The Princess Stakes Murder

Kin Platt

Random House: New York

Library of Congress Cataloging in Publication Data

Platt, Kin.
    The Princess Stakes murder.

    I. Title.
PZ4.P7196Pr   [PS3566.L29]   813′.5′4   72–10095
ISBN 0–394–48147–X

First Edition

to John F. Marion

The Princess Stakes Murder

One

The tune is nostalgic and familiar. The old recording by Crosby. They play it before the first and after the last race. It's corny and it gets you.

> Where the turf meets the surf
> Down at old Del Mar,
> Take a plane, take a train, take a car;
> There's a smile on every face
> And a winner in each race
> Where the turf meets the surf at Del Mar.

I was there on Labor Day along with about thirty thousand dedicated track nuts. They were running the Princess Stakes. For three-year-olds and up, fillies and mares. Six furlongs for $100,000.

Willie Rich had called me the night before to tell me he was riding Calamity. She was a good filly and that would be the next to closing race on the card, the eighth. I got there earlier because Del Mar is the kind of track that looks good even without the horses running. It's flat, set in the bowl of a pretty valley rimmed by purple mountains, caressed by soft sea breezes. No one hurries around the grounds. It's all relaxed and easy, the way people and horse racing used to be.

Saratoga, old and venerable, was where the better two-year-olds were sent to prove themselves in the East. Old Del Mar, not as old and gracious as its big sister, does the same for the young hopefuls in the West. Most of them are maidens or unraced, and only their trainers and owners know how fast they are. It's one of the tougher tracks to handicap.

The Del Mar season opens late July and runs through early September. They run a few tune-up races for the major stake events. There's the Futurity for colts and geldings. The Debutante for fillies. The one that brought me out—the Princess Stakes.

The architecture around the track puts you back into the romantic era of old Spanish missions and California ranchos. You think of dons and doñas, hidalgos, gentle priests and Indians. You can get murdered trying to pick a winner and it's like having it happen to you in a church or cathedral. It's a hundred miles back to Los Angeles, but you can see the ocean most of the way. Del Mar comforts its losers.

I sat looking down over the freshly painted green seats at the colorful moving crowd. The infield was raked and immaculate. The hills beyond were peaceful, rolling gently above the valley. The sun was warm, the skies blue. Willie Rich hadn't bothered with any of the details the night before, when he called me in Santa Monica.

His voice filtered through his typical tough gravel, no giveaway that he was a little man. "What's with you lately?" he had asked. "You don't follow the ponies any more?"

"It's a hobby I can't afford lately, Willie. I read about them the morning after, in the sports pages."

"I'm riding a good filly tomorrow, Max."

"That wouldn't be Calamity?"

He laughed. "So you can still read. Why don't you take a ride down and see us go?" He sensed my hesitation and added quickly, "It's the eighth race. Post time for the opener is two. You've got plenty of time to be there." Then, "Besides, I want to talk to you."

4

"Anything special?"

"It'll keep. You coming?"

"I'll be there."

"Right on. I'll make it worth the trip."

"Any time you're on a good one, Willie, it's worth the trip. By the way, how's married life?"

"Remind me to tell you about it. How are things with you? You still looking for people?"

"Only when they kill people."

"That's the best way to go. I'll see you, Max."

The Labor Day crowd was on its feet for the Princess Stakes, screaming and shouting. Pretty little things punched their consorts on the arm, jumped up and down and squealed excitedly.

Calamity broke well out of the starting gate heading for the inside rail. Willie Rich placed her just off the brisk early pace to the far turn, some three lengths in front of the tightly packed field. Willie touched the pretty filly and Calamity had the lead when the pacesetter and favorite, Humble Hilda, hung. Calamity held off a challenge by Sister Sally at the top of the stretch, and pulled away from the pregnant mare to win by a length. The time was 1:08—only one-fifth off Crazy Kid's track record.

The crowd went wild. It's always nice to win and I felt good inside. It was a big win all around. For Calamity, for the Black Oak stable of owner Tyler Clayton, for trainer Cap Abbott, and a bigger one for Willie. He now had 547 career stake wins, only seven away from the all-time record of Eddie Arcaro's posted 554.

I collected my winnings and went up to the Turf Club bar. I had a drink and waited for Willie. I waited, had a few more. He still didn't show. They were lining them up for the nightcap ninth and I was still alone. I knew Willie didn't have a mount, was through for the day. I went down to find out why he was stiffing me.

A lot of played-out birds were sprawled on the grass

working on their forms and charts. The turf handicappers were busy inside their vans printing up the cards listing their winners for the day. I went over to the jock club building and braced the big tough security guard hanging outside.

"I'm looking for Willie Rich."

He looked me over slowly, shook his head. "Sorry, Mac. You're too late."

"What do you mean?" I asked.

"About fifteen minutes ago," he said. "He left."

"Left? Left where?"

He wagged his thumb toward the parking lot beyond the paddock. "He left the park. Right after the eighth. He weighed in with his saddle, came back, showered, got dressed and left."

"Anybody with him?"

"Nope."

I felt let down. "My name's Roper. Did he leave any message?"

His lips pursed and he looked regretful. "Sorry, Mac. He didn't tell me nothing. Just left, like I said."

I found my heap in the lot and tootled back to L.A. through heavy traffic. I'd won a bundle on the classy filly Calamity and regretted not having been able to celebrate it properly with Willie. He hadn't stressed any urgency about our getting together, he was a very popular jock, and I could imagine a great many reasons for his cutting out so abruptly and not meeting me. But the Del Mar season had a lot to run yet and I knew we'd get together easily enough before it was over.

I couldn't believe it when I got a call about two in the morning from Allie Riegel, another old friend, who handles the track-security detail for Del Mar. He put it to me right on the nose. They had just found Willie Rich floating in his swimming pool at his home in Escondido. He wasn't wearing swim trunks. He was dead, of course.

It seemed a hell of a way to celebrate such a nice winning day.

Two

The next morning was hot and humid and my jaws ached. I drove the San Diego Freeway south mechanically, my mind circling the fact of Willie Rich's death endlessly without resolution. We had seen little of each other the past few years, and although we had spoken and exchanged brief sallies, there were too many gaps between for anything but futile conjecture. Two hours later, I wheeled into the Del Mar official parking lot across from the old Bing Crosby Hall memorial building, hoping for facts.

It was too early for track activity. I could feel the pall hanging over the jock club quarter. State troopers and local fuzz were beating down the hay in stalls and paddocks. A group of well-dressed and solemn bigwigs filed out of Allie's office.

Allie Riegel had been a top government agent. As chief of the Del Mar Thoroughbred security, he was as tough as a man given that slot could be and still remain human. He stood big as a mountain and wasn't any more corruptible. He was balder than I remembered him, his deeply tanned face lined with worry.

He didn't smile when I came in or say hello and I didn't expect him to. We looked each other over stonily, a couple of emotionally bankrupt cases.

His office was quiet and cool, far removed from the hay burners at the far end. A lot of paper work littered his desk, but he didn't have to look at any notes to fill me in.

"Penny found him," he said for openers.

That would be Penny Rich. Mrs. Willie Rich.

"I don't think it's been too good there," Allie added.

Willie hadn't asked me when he married her two years earlier. She was young and pretty without a brain in her little head but the kind of figure to help you forget it. Willie had been riding hard for twenty years and for him, I suppose, she was a teeny-bopper delight, worth all the grief she had to give him.

"She got home a little after midnight," Allie was saying. "She said she'd had a few drinks and thought it would be fun to take a dip in the pool before retiring. She went in with all her clothes on. She came up out of her dive and found Willie at the other end of the pool. He still had his clothes on, too, and she thought it was a gag and pretty funny, at first. Then, after she saw he was dead and had stopped screaming, she called me.

"I got there with our track physician, Dr. Taniguchi, at one. He figured Willie was dead two hours. Roughly, between ten and eleven. No visible marks of violence."

Allie bit the end off a fresh cigar, spat it out and looked up at me.

"You don't need any," I said.

Allie lit up, blew smoke and rubbed his bald dome.

"You don't need any if you can hold a man's head under water," I said.

"You're saying somebody did it to Willie?"

"Why should he take himself out? He had Longden's record for career wins and was only seven short of Arcaro's record for stakes. I thought he always wanted that one, too."

Allie looked at the ash on his long stogy. "Anything you *know?*"

"He stiffed me yesterday. Called me the night before the Princess Stakes and told me he was riding a good filly. He

8

said he wanted to talk to me about something, but it would keep. I had a few drinks at the Turf Club bar after the eighth and waited, but Willie never showed. That's been our usual meeting place. I checked with your security guard outside the jock club and he said Willie had gone. He didn't leave word for me. They were running the ninth when I left."

Allie shook off the question in my eyes. "I didn't see him take off and don't know where he went."

"Probably not home," I said. "I've had the feeling you mention, that all was not well there with him and Penny."

Allie sighed. "You feel good," he said.

I studied my watch. "The ninth went off at six. You found Willie at one, less two hours of life. All we need—five hours to fill in. Somebody must have seen him."

"Sure. The guy at his swimming pool who watched Willie drown."

"You're buying that?"

"Well, why the hell do you think I brought you into it?" Allie snapped.

"I liked Willie," I said. "You didn't bring me into anything, Al. You only told me about what happened."

"Okay, okay. So we both liked Willie. A lot of others did, too. What we need is a line on those who didn't."

"I've been out of touch lately," I said. "The mob never could reach Willie and they knew it. Let's start with around here. Track personnel. The other jocks, trainers, owners, the lot."

Allie handed me a sheet of paper off his desk. He added three more stapled sheets. "You'll find everybody there who works or breathes at Del Mar, including me."

I looked it over briefly. "Including transients? Don't you have a lot of out-of-towners now for the season?"

Allie scowled. "They're down there, too. Only not in the same detail. You can start by looking them over. If you want more, we'll get it for you."

I nodded. "Let's see if we agree about some of the group around him. Was Penny giving him hell?"

9

Allie rubbed his jaw. "Whatever gave you that idea?"

"But he wouldn't kill himself over that. I can't see Penny wanting him out of the way either. He let her roam, didn't he? And he was always worth more booting home the winners. Why would she want him dead?"

"Maybe she wanted the pool all to herself when she got home late at night," Allie suggested.

I turned the page. "Tyler Clayton. He owns Calamity and several others. I've heard he's a very wealthy man. Anything else you can tell me about him?"

"He got me my spot here. I run security. Apart from that example of clearheaded rational thinking, Clayton's a mean, tough, pigheaded man. Wants what he wants when he wants it."

"That's fine," I said. "Do you give it to him?"

"He'd throw me out on my ear if I did. That's the way he operates, Max. Hot and cold."

"Willie been his rider for long?"

"About five years."

"So he made a lot of money for Clayton."

"Sure. But we already agreed Clayton doesn't need it."

"I think I'll run over and see Clayton. Maybe I'll find out what a very rich man like that really needs."

Allie scratched his ear with his telephone. "You starting with him? I'll let him know I sent you."

"No," I said. "With Penny."

He put the phone back. "Okay, sport. Offhand, though, I figure Penny doesn't need anything either."

"I know," I said. "But I've seen pictures of Tyler Clayton. Penny is a lot easier on the eyes."

"There's just one thing," Allie said.

I walked back and waited.

"Clayton's daughter is missing," he said.

"Missing since when?"

His shrug was negligible. "Yesterday."

"What time yesterday?"

"Noon."

"How old would that daughter be?"

"Over twenty-one," Allie said. "Maybe twenty-two."

"They do that at that age, I hear," I said. "Is Clayton worried?"

Allie looked out his window and showed me his profile. "Not too much."

"You want me to be?" I asked.

Allie stretched and yawned. He'd probably been up all night. "You know horse racing."

"The sport of kings," I said. "Tell me, is this missing heiress pretty?"

"Name me one who isn't."

I shook my head. "I didn't come down here to find a missing heiress, no matter how pretty. I'm wound up about Willie."

"I know," he said. "That's why I fed you a little more. *Cherchez la femme.*"

"Was there a threat, Allie? Did Willie have to throw it or else?"

He pretended to look at his notes. "I don't have that information here."

I tried to remember the card in the eighth. "Who was the mare that ran second? She went off at thirty to one, didn't she?"

"Sister Sally. That's Mrs. Clayton's horse."

I stared at him stupidly. "Mrs. Clayton's mare was running against her husband's filly Calamity, with Willie up?"

Allie nodded and riffled through his desk papers looking for his lighter. "I was hoping that would strike you as odd."

"It's not odd, it's fishy." I tried a few mental exercises that led me farther afield. "Was Mrs. Clayton's daughter here yesterday for the Princess?"

"I don't know," Allie said. He found his lighter and relit his cigar. "Incidentally, Pam Clayton is Tyler's daughter, not the present Mrs. Clayton's."

"Pam is the missing heiress?"

"Very pretty, too," Allie said. "A knockout. You look pretty mad now but I'll bet you wind up thanking me."

"You mean, if she's still alive."

Allie threw his hands apart. "That's what I meant when I said—"

"*Cherchez la femme.*"

"Keep in touch," Allie said as I stomped out.

Three

The narrow winding tarback curves of Black Mountain Road threading around Gonzales Canyon permitted occasional glimpses of stately white houses behind the lush avocado and citrus ranches. The gentle rolling hills of Escondido were a quiet contrast to the screaming Labor Day turnout the previous day at old Del Mar.

Willie's spread was at the end of a humpbacked dirt and gravel lane. It looked expensive and it was. But winning jocks ride for ten percent of the take and Willie had booted home many millions for his owners over the years, and could afford the layout. I couldn't tell how happy he'd been there, and maybe if he hadn't swallowed too much water, I might have known.

The flashy little blonde at the far end of the pool wearing very little of a strawberry bikini was the other expensive bit of the landscaping. She was sitting under a colorful poolside umbrella sipping out of a tall frosted glass. She was wearing dark tinted sunglasses and looking out toward the mountains. She was smoking a joint and I couldn't tell if she was happy or sad.

"Mrs. Rich," I said. "My name's Max Roper. Maybe Willie mentioned my name. We were friends."

The dark glasses reluctantly left the distant hills and

swung in my direction. She nodded coolly without expression. "Christ! Everybody that calls says he was a friend of Willie's."

"Sounds reasonable," I said. "He was a popular guy."

"Yeah," she said. "I'll remind him when he comes in."

She looked like a shapely little girl and her voice had that same odd singsong quality, but she packed her own kind of venom, flat and purposeful. Either it was there all the time hidden under the soft, cuddly bunny cover, or a little too much living had rubbed her raw.

"Can you tell me anything about it?" I asked.

"What's to tell? He's dead." She extended a shapely tanned leg and kicked it toward the pool. "Drowned in his own goddam swimming pool, for Christ's sake."

I pulled out a chair and covered it. "Allie Riegel told me. We're trying to find out who had it in for Willie."

She tilted her cute little head. "Why? Is somebody offering a reward?"

I nodded to the smoking joint in her fingers. "Maybe if you put that away, you'll be able to talk sense. I imagine the police have been out here asking you the same questions."

She took another bite out of it, held it deep, and let it out slowly. "So what?" she said scornfully. "They're fuzz. Who the hell are you?"

I flipped open my wallet. "I'm a private investigator. Riegel wants me to do the job for the Del Mar Club. I'm in it because Willie was a friend and I want who knocked him off."

She laughed. "That's a crock. For all anybody knows, Willie did it himself."

"Drowned himself? Why would he do that?"

She shook her head slowly and giggled. "It sure beats me. Why don't you ask him?"

"Too much grieving isn't healthy," I said. "You ought to get your mind off it. Do you really think Willie drowned himself?"

"How the hell should I know?" she said. "He didn't tell me what went on in his mind. He didn't tell me nothing. Like

14

he knew everything and I was the world's prize dope. Like I hardly ever saw him except in the sack, and not too damn much of that, either, if you want to know." She tittered and added in a cockney bit, "If you ask me, dearie, 'e lost it all on the 'orses, 'e did."

I leaned toward her. "Okay, so you had differences. A man doesn't kill himself just because he's got a rotten marriage, not anybody who was top of his field like Willie. If he wanted out, he could have afforded a divorce, no matter how much your lawyers wanted."

"What's it to you?" she said. "What's in it for you? You private eyes work for money, don't you? Well, it's not worth a dime to me, how it happened or who did it to who." She rubbed her joint out savagely in the ashtray. "For all I know, the little bastard had it coming. Do me a favor, will you, and get lost."

I stood up. "Maybe I'll drop in on you again when you're over your grief. I was hoping you might give me a line on Willie's enemies. Maybe somebody was trying to pressure him into something. Maybe they were worrying him."

" 'They'? Who's 'they'?"

"I was hoping you'd tell me, Mrs. Rich."

"All I can tell you is get lost," she said.

"I'll find out who did it and how it happened," I said. "It'll do your heart good."

"Go to hell." She pushed her sunglasses back and her blue eyes squinted angrily at me. "And don't bother coming back. I got enough headaches without you."

I walked back the same way I'd come in, following the pool terrace to my car. I glanced quickly at the end of the pool where she claimed to have found Willie. It looked peaceful and innocent. As I approached my car, a man was just getting out of his, parked alongside. He was husky, dark-haired and pallid, nicely dressed, wearing an open shirt and silk bandanna, Hollywood style. His features were rough and crude but didn't come anywhere near his real personality. I knew him as a hood called Johnny Cashio. He was a reliable enforcer for the mob, very cute with the knife. He worked free-lance, and like Willie Rich, Cashio was offered big percentages and payoffs.

We didn't know each other on sight. Cashio brushed shoulders with me as he walked by and flipped his hand in salute. I was relieved to notice there wasn't a knife in it.

Four

The Black Mountain Road looped around southwest to Rancho Santa Fe, a serene valley catering to the extreme tastes of millionaires who liked their furbishings on the dull side. A lot of horse people lived there, many of them the true-lovers-of-the-thoroughbred breed who liked their pictures taken in the winner's circle. Tyler C. Clayton was the one I wanted to see. He was the owner of a twelve-horse stable which included the filly, Calamity, Willie had brought home for his last race, a successful participant in the sport of racing thoroughbreds. He had made it in oil, as good a way as any of assuring one's life style would never be circumscribed by lack of funds. His winning stable, the Black Oak Farm, brought him an extra few million a year, which, as Allie Riegel had admitted, Clayton didn't really need.

I parked my heap in a driveway big enough to be called a parking lot and walked up some stone steps and lifted the heavy bronze door knocker and let it fall.

A slim, pretty dark-haired girl in a domestic's shift opened the big heavy door. "Is Mr. Clayton home?" I asked.

She looked me over and smiled and didn't ask me what I was selling. She stepped back gracefully. "Come in. Who shall I say, please?" Her accent sounded Scandinavian but her roots looked solid brunette. I told her who I was and mentioned Allie Riegel's name. She smiled again, and nodded. "Oh, yes. Just a moment, if you please, I'll see."

The hall was high with a cool tile flooring and good dark wood on the walls. The furnishings looked elegant but I liked better the way the Scandinavian maid walked.

She returned in a moment beckoning. "Please, this way."

"Thank you, Pauli," a heavy voice boomed. I stepped into a light spacious book-lined study. "Yes, Mr. Roper. What can I do for you?"

I blinked in the dazzling morning light and then smiled when I saw him. He was simply too big to be missed in any-size room. He stood an easy six five or six and would have brought the needle of any scale to its knees close to two five oh. The walls were covered with delicate prints of horses, and there were small sculptured equine figurines all along the borders of his bookcase and on his desk and end tables.

"It's about Willie Rich. I'm a private investigator. Willie was a friend of mine. I'd like to find out what happened."

His grip did justice to his bulk. "So would I, dammit. So would I. Riegel sent you over, did he? That's fine, sir. I'll be happy to help you any way I can. I liked Willie. Goddam good jockey, too. You just ask what you want. Don't cut any corners here. I'm grateful to you for coming, sir."

He asked me what I drank, turned to a sideboard, splashed it into a large glass, and put it in my hand. He then poured himself one and lifted his glass to me. I returned his salute and we stood fixed for a moment with arms outstretched like men at some crazy ritual. I gave it all the moment called for and then let it into my throat and he did the same. He whipped open a fancy cigar box lined with copper and I picked out a slim long panetella. I bit off the end, he had the flame ready, and I took two long gentle puffs and was convinced I liked his style, his courtesy and his stock. He indicated a soft chair and I let myself sink into it and had another belt while I looked him over.

Tyler Clayton looked to be in his sixties, a rough-looking

man who appeared still able to hold his own with any of the roustabouts in the oil-rigging game. A lot of good rough-and-tumble fighters come out of the oil fields, hard men with big hands and heavily muscled bodies. Clayton had probably put on some weight but was deep-chested and big enough to carry it well. His voice traced a pattern I couldn't get a fix on. He sounded like a Deep Southern gentleman, with some Texas panhandle rubbed on. I guessed he'd moved around when he was growing up and assimilated whatever each neighborhood offered.

I explained about missing Willie the previous day and asked if he'd seen him. He shook his big head regretfully. "Not after we posed for the picture in the winner's circle, son," he rumbled. "Willie still had to go back and weigh in, and that was the last I saw of him. I left immediately after, myself; didn't have anything going in the ninth."

"Do you think Willie drowned himself, Mr. Clayton?"

"Hell, no! Why would he do a thing like that? He was still a winning rider, good for a lot of years, making big money."

"That's the way I see it," I said. "I've just been over to see Mrs. Rich."

"Oh?"

"She wasn't helpful. I suppose you know it wasn't exactly a happy marriage."

His shaking head rejected the idea. "Now, hold on, son. I don't know if I'd go that far. I've seen them together. Maybe it wasn't the best for each of them, but I don't know if it was all that bad. Least I never heard Willie complain."

I lifted my glass. "Talk to Penny. Maybe she'll make it up for him and help you change your mind."

He shook his grizzled head again. "No, doggone it. I can't do that. It's not my business to pry and stir up troubled feelings. Now, you're a professional. If you say it seemed that way, then I'll be of an open mind and listen. But what's done is done, and you can see that."

I stared, surprised to find him so pliable. "Okay, it's

done. Maybe you can give me a line on some of Willie's enemies."

His sad slate eyes were blank. "Enemies? Why, Willie didn't have a one! Everybody liked Willie—everybody!"

"Not everybody, Mr. Clayton. If Willie didn't commit suicide, there has to be the guy who held his head under water. I don't think he'd qualify as a friend."

Clayton ironed some creases off the back of his thick neck with one large hand. "I've been over it with the police. Whoever did this terrible thing wasn't seen, apparently. He didn't leave any tracks. I couldn't think of a motive for them, and I can't do any better for you. I'm sorry."

"We'll get one," I said. "Have you received any threats about Calamity—any of your horses?"

He looked surprised. "Threats?" It must have been a word with which he was very unfamiliar.

"Gamblers. Coercion. Sometimes they want to pick their own horse to win."

He grinned wildly and rubbed his short-cropped grizzled hair. "That'd be the day, son. I'd like to see them try it." He clapped his big hands together and rubbed them, then broke off and leveled a thick forefinger at me. "Del Mar is a clean track, son, and we aim to keep it that way. I've been around horses a long time. I know all about that hanky-panky. That's why I brought Allie Riegel in, if you're interested. He's a mighty tough customer, I'll tell you. Sure we got gamblers. That's what horse racing is all about. But we run a clean operation and nobody cuts himself in. I mean nobody."

I shrugged it off. "Jockeys can be reached and tapped. Not every owner and trainer is as big and tough and rich as you. It's been done before."

I wondered what business Johnny Cashio had with Penny Rich. Given his connections, it didn't look right. Especially so soon after Willie's death.

Clayton was on his feet giving a pretty good imitation of an angry bear. I was hoping he didn't get himself too worked up and throw me through some of that expensive woodwork.

He stalked the room cocking his head at each classy thoroughbred hanging on his walls. He ground to a halt finally and stared out the picture window.

"Maybe," he said gruffly. "I'll give you that. Sure as hell it's happened. Everybody wants money and can be reached for a killing. I'm no fool. But that's history. It doesn't tie up with Willie. He rode ten winners the past week. All pretty good horses. Nobody stumbled at the gate for him or lagged out or pulled up. Nobody made a killing on anything under him. He lost a few, too, and those were expected. He got beat by better horses. We run a lot of two-year-olds here at Del Mar and there isn't much of a line on them. Some of the better three-year-old fillies and colts are still maidens, too, and can bring a pretty good price. But there hasn't been any big jump in the tote board odds and far as we know there hasn't been any killing."

"You left out one," I said. "Willie's."

He relit his long cigar and eyed me sideways as he clamped down on it. "You know," he said, "you kind of remind me of myself. Like you're used to trouble. Used to handling it, I mean."

"I've had my lumps," I said.

"I'm talking about trouble," Clayton said. "Real trouble. You're not a family man, I take it."

"Never touch the stuff."

A woman appeared in the open doorway. She was a strawberry blonde in her late thirties or slightly past, quite beautiful, wearing expensive casual threads. She hesitated when she saw Clayton had company.

The ex-roustabout looked up politely. "Yes, Monica?"

Her voice was a whiskey growl, low and urgent. "I'll wait until you're through, Tyler. I didn't know you had a visitor."

"It's all right, my dear." He extended his arm and gently tugged her in. "My wife, Mr. Roper." He turned to her. "Mr. Roper is a private detective investigating Willie's death. Allie Reigel sent him over."

She nodded, then put her hand gracefully to her throat. It was a small gesture, but that involuntary move suddenly sent me chasing along the wheels of memory. I was certain I knew her.

"Perhaps we should speak to Mr. Roper, Tyler, since he's here now. And if Mr. Riegel recommended him."

Clayton scowled and waved his big hands. "Now, Monica. Hold on. I don't think there's any need."

Her head tilted back and her green eyes glowed. "I'm sorry to disagree, darling. But she is your daughter and I'm worried."

I managed to look blankly from one to the other. Clayton stood rigid and uncomfortable.

"Please, Tyler," she said softly. "Surely it can't hurt."

He chewed on his lip for a while, and then suddenly his pique dissolved. The whole scene looked phony as hell.

"Okay," he growled. "Go ahead, if you feel you have to. Go on. Spill it."

I gave Mrs. Clayton my gentle reassuring level-with-me look.

"It's Tyler's daughter, Pamela," she said huskily. "She's missing."

I looked surprised. "Missing? Since when?"

She glanced at Clayton. He frowned, shook her off, and let her carry the ball. "Since yesterday."

I said how sorry I was to hear that and asked how old the missing girl was, and she told me. Twenty-two.

Clayton shrugged and got back into the act. "Just turned twenty-two. June."

"Do you have any idea where she was going?"

It was Monica Clayton's turn to hesitate and think. She did it more gracefully than I. "She had a beauty parlor appointment yesterday. That's all I can tell you."

I had pencil and notebook at the ready. "Where?"

"It's a beauty and health spa—in Poway."

"The name of the place?"

She cleared her throat. "The Gilded Cuckoo."

I wrote it down. "What time was her appointment?"

"Ten-thirty yesterday morning."

"Did she keep it?"

She hesitated and did magic *ninja* finger exercises, the *kuji-kiri.* "I'm not sure. I know she left early enough."

"Did you check with them—at the Gilded Cuckoo?"

"Yes. They said she never arrived."

"Have you notified the police?"

She looked at Clayton. A lot of the ruddiness had seeped out of his face, exposing deep furrows. He stared out his window. She shook her head negative.

"Any particular reason, Mrs. Clayton?"

Her green eyes were haunted, holding a lot of trouble. She looked at me mute and helplessly. My mind was still back-pedaling for her, but she wasn't where I was looking.

I turned over my wrist watch. "It's only twenty-four hours. She's over twenty-one. She might walk in the door any minute with a reasonable explanation."

"Yes—I suppose—"

"Young girls," I said lightly, "they like to worry their parents."

They accepted the statement.

"A lot of them these days are on drugs," I said.

A repressed growl was winning over Clayton's throat.

"Any particular reason you're not telling the police, Mr. Clayton?" I asked.

He shook his head, stone-faced.

I remembered Willie Rich had ridden for this man for a few years. Daughters of the very rich are not supposed to play with the hired help. "Do you think there's any tie-up?" I asked. "I mean, your daughter disappearing on the same day Willie Rich got murdered?"

Tyler Clayton was bent over his desk, arms out and braced wide apart, his deeply trenched face bleak and forbidding.

"What's that you're saying, mister?" he growled.

I looked into his narrowed glinting eyes, searching for a

ray of good will without luck. "I'm not trying to worry you," I said. "But that's the line the police would take. They'd be looking for some tie-up. A threat maybe if Willie didn't pull a horse when he was told to." I put my cigar down next to his in the big ashtray. "But you'd have had some warning, I imagine, if they were trying that kind of coercion. You're telling me nothing happened, is that correct?"

Clayton's jaw sagged as if I'd hit him with one of my better punches. "Are you suggesting—are you saying my kid's been snatched—kidnapped?"

I waved my hands soothingly. "No. But it's the line the police might take."

He pushed himself off the desk and straightened up. "Just find her," he said, breathing hard, "and stop asking so many goddam fool questions." His hard eyes raked me. "I don't believe a damn word you're saying, and that's the last you'll get out of me."

Instead of throwing me out, he went himself.

I watched him go and then turned to the gracefully swaying strawberry-blond matron. "I'm sorry," I said. "Do you have a picture of the girl?"

She smiled gently, pointing past my head. "She's over there."

I turned, puzzled, seeing nothing. There was a soft murmur and she was gliding past me in a smooth sinuous motion, brushing by so closely that her delicate perfume was strong in my nostrils. I tingled where she had touched the fibers of my suit.

"Here." She had picked a silver frame off the large desk. The girl in the picture didn't look very much like Tyler Clayton's daughter. She was fresh-looking, smiling, blue-eyed and beautiful. All you'd ever want to see in a blonde.

I remembered Allie Riegel's summation. A knockout.

When I looked up, Monica Clayton was studying my face, her eyes hooded, expressionless. There seemed more behind it than a casual appraisal, but I couldn't figure it out any more than I could get over the strong feeling I had that we'd met somewhere.

"I'll try to find her," I said. She bowed her head. "By the way, was that your mare Sister Sally who got beat by Calamity, your husband's filly?"

Her voice was husky and mocking. "Calamity didn't beat her. Willie did."

"But that wasn't reason enough for you to kill him," I said.

"No, it wasn't," she said.

The dark-haired Scandinavian maid let me out. I didn't ask her any questions because she smelled strongly of soap and water and I wanted to hold that scent of delicate perfume in my nostrils a little longer.

Five

The Rancho Santa Fe road traveling east had a lot of dipsy-doodle curves and canyons, but I didn't see any fastback green Mustangs piled in a heap at the bottom of any of them. The run was ten minutes to the Gilded Cuckoo in Poway and whoever named the spa wasn't kidding. Business in narcissism was booming, judging from the spacious network of low-set buildings scattered with an indulgent architectural hand. The main center dome was gilded, as were the doors. There weren't any paying clients outside, so it was safe to assume the cuckoos were in. There were fountains and waterfalls, pools and porticoes, riding stables, tennis and volleyball courts, and a jogging track with banked turns. Out-of-town spas were good for kicking habits, with drugs and booze high up on the list, followed by weight and body conditioning for cosmetic vanity. They were good places to get away from your husband, or wife, or family, or the FBI, and sometimes even gambling syndicate enforcers. Looking at this opulent haven for losers, I could only speculate on what had induced the young and beautiful Pam Clayton to come here for remedial treatment. There were any number of good hair stylists closer to home. But then she could have been fighting weight, going for the slim-trim course.

A tawny-haired young thing with big gray eyes and a

very short skirt was explaining the curriculum to me, leaning over her desk distractingly as she stabbed her finger at the colored folder. "Besides that, there's ballet, Yoga, massage, skin treatment, gym and swimming pool exercises. But what we stress here mostly is Body Contrology Rhythm."

"Yes, I see," I said.

She handed me a sheet of paper listing courses and phases in small type, a standard application contract. "Just fill in what you're interested in most. It's only a formality. The director will then interview you and help you fashion your courses and schedule." She looked me over disinterestedly. "What is it, a weight problem?"

I sucked in my gut and tried to pretend her question was of no consequence. "I guess so." I looked toward the blank door behind her. "Perhaps if I could see your director now?"

"But you haven't filled out the form."

"I can't decide—it's too complicated for me." I waved my hands helplessly. "Maybe your director could help."

She smiled. "I know your problem. You're shy."

I shifted my weight, shuffled my feet, and looked embarrassed. She picked up her phone. "I'll see if he can work you in today. I'm not sure, without an appointment. But there's nothing to be embarrassed over, you know. A lot of middle-aged men come here."

I gave her a sadder, fatter and older glance. "Really?"

She giggled. "Some of them are worse than women. You'd be surprised." She whispered into the mouthpiece. "A new client, Mr. Glendon," she said. Her eyes flickered to my relaxed and expanding midriff. "Would you be a live-in, do you think?"

I said I wasn't sure.

"What name, please?"

I told her, she relayed the information, listened and hung up. She smiled happily. "Wonderful! Mr. Glendon will see you." She pointed to another door to my right. "Through that door, Mr. Roper. He'll be right with you."

"Thanks," I said and started for it.

"Remember, don't be shy," she said. "We're here to help you."

"I'll try," I told her and went through the door.

The chamber was small, air-conditioned, decorated with subtle soothing restraint. There were folders on a small copy of a Hepplewhite table that gracefully followed the curves of the master's style. Available courses were listed without the humdrum and niggardly detail of prices. A George Glendon was down as the director. Another inner door opened and he pranced in.

"Mr. Roper? I'm George Glendon, director of our little sanctuary. How might I help you?"

He was moon-faced, frisky and thick-shouldered. Average height with small hands and feet. He looked younger than the fifty-odd his eyes said he was. I could see him at home in a kitchen or patting down a bed, fluffing a pillow.

I waved the circular helplessly. "I—I'm not sure. I've heard so much about this place, and I thought—well, you know—I sit around a lot." I tapped the apparently obvious midriff. "I like to eat." He was studying me coolly. "Drink, too, of course."

He smiled confidently. "Don't we all?" he said heartily. "But then, we do have to pay the piper for it, don't we?"

I sagged and nodded dispiritedly.

"No problem, really. You may have let yourself go to pot, so to speak, over the years, abusing your system." He eyed the cigarette in my hand sternly. "But we can reverse the process and put you in proper shape again. We've a lot of good people here, dedicated to their work."

"I don't know," I said. "How long would it take?"

He shrugged. "It depends on your cooperation, of course. How important it is to you to regain your youth and vigor. We can help you get it back, if you really want it."

I looked glum. "Exercise?"

"Yes, and besides that your body is pushed and pounded into shape. Oh, your muscles may scream and tell you

28

they're being tortured, but they'll respond and firm up. As for stomachs, they may complain at our rigorously imposed low-calorie diet, but they shrink." He patted his sides proudly. "Believe me, they do."

I looked at his flat belly enviously. "Is that the Body Contrology course?"

He smiled. "Yes. We think in terms of restructuring the body, rather than merely weight loss. You'll see inches rather than pounds disappear."

I patted my own sides lightly, thinking fat.

"Body Contrology Rhythm is the closest thing to the dance. It develops long flexible muscles. You are taught to control the mind, body, spirit and breath through self-discipline."

I looked at the folder in my hand. "How much—?"

"We believe in brain, body and soul all stimulated and fused into creativity and love in order to attain the perfect body."

"It sounds very good," I said. "But how long—?"

"There's Plan A," he said dreamily, "a course of approximately twelve lessons."

I chewed on my lip. "Do you think that would be enough?"

He took a lithe step to the side and had the inner door open. "Why don't we take a look around? You'll be able to decide far easier after you've seen our facilities."

I hesitated momentarily and then followed him through the door.

The corridor was wide and well-carpeted. He nodded briskly toward closed doors on either side. Some had small glass partitions on top. "Beauty salon," he said disdainfully. "We've better things to offer you."

I caught glimpses of women and some men in chairs hovered over by attendants. Some were wearing cylinders over their heads. I saw a lot of filled chairs and some cute-looking hair stylists. I wondered if I didn't need a haircut.

"This way."

A brick-studded path led to another wing. "Skin salon," Glendon said, tossing his head.

"Oh, brother," I said carelessly.

Glendon stopped. He peered closely at my face. "You'd be surprised, Mr. Roper. We have some marvelous nourishing and moisturizing creams to help you fend off those encroaching age lines. We have in Dr. Powers a most experienced and skillful dermatologist."

I rubbed my cheek. It didn't feel worse than usual.

"Here. Feel mine." He thrust his chin toward me, raised my hand, and placed it lightly on his face. "There's the proof. I give my face and skin constant protection, you see."

"But," I protested weakly, "you're—well, younger."

He smiled deprecatingly. "Past forty."

"No."

"Yes. And I have Dr. Powers and his assistants to thank. Deep pore cleansing. You'd be surprised what it can do."

I was back to my own face, comparing. "Well. Maybe."

He was in stride again. "You'll make your own decision. But they do marvelous work with ozone treatment and face vacuuming." He laughed. "Don't worry. That's the least of your worries now."

A more important one was how I was going to get Glendon to backtrack to Pam Clayton and her canceled appointment, or get to see his books. Meanwhile I was interested in the guided tour of the spa. It seemed the kind of place where a person with sufficient funds could hide out successfully for a long time.

" 'Self-love, my liege, is not so vile as self-neglect,' " Glendon said. He smiled at my eye-batting as I struggled for comprehension. "*Henry the Fifth*, by William Shakespeare. I think it should be inscribed over our doors, don't you?"

"It couldn't hurt."

"Oh, that reminds me." He threw open a door to a small building and motioned me inside. He walked briskly through a narrow carpeted corridor and then stopped. The upper part of the dark-gray wall was glass. "Take a look through here. A see-through mirror. We're invisible from the other side."

The room was small and featured a long white couch. A man was lying on it stripped but for trunks. Contact pads ran from his body to a machine. At the machine was a white-coated operator. The man at the machine flipped a switch. The face of the man on the white couch contorted. The pads covering his body jiggled. His arms, shoulders, back, stomach and leg muscles went into massive contractions.

I looked at Glendon, wondering if he had recently enlisted the son of Dr. Fu Manchu to assist at the Cuckoo.

"There is no pain," Glendon was saying. "His face is contorted because it's the body's natural reaction. His muscles are being contracted rhythmically at five-second impulses."

I watched the man flinch and squirm. Nobody could convince me the patient wasn't being killed before my eyes.

"There is no pain," Glendon was saying, "because the electrical impulses of the machine by-pass the motor nervous system."

I nodded, unconvinced.

"It's an electronic device called the isotron."

"What's it for?"

"Space-age fitness. A twenty-minute treatment is roughly the equivalent of two hours of vigorous weight lifting."

I watched the man suffer painlessly a while longer, and then the operator flipped his switch and the man lay still. The operator walked over to the couch, removed the contact pads, and the man stirred and sat up. He looked big and strong enough to pick the white-coated attendant up and break him over his muscle-contracting machine but he didn't. Maybe he enjoyed it.

"Oh, yes," Glendon was saying as he stepped back, "a lot of weight people are using it. One man went from three hundred fifty to four sixty-five in the Olympic weight press. You see, it can contract your muscles far beyond what your mind can make them do. That's what makes it so fantastic."

I could imagine a lot of unsavory space-age rogues bending minds and wills with this obviously patented device. I knew what my muscles could do, and I didn't like the idea of any machine telling them they could do more.

I didn't want Glendon to think I was unappreciative of the arts and skills behind his spa. "How much for the muscle bender?"

"Six months of treatments costs five hundred dollars. All it takes is three times a week, for twenty-minute sessions."

"What happens if the man working the machine falls asleep during a session?"

Glendon laughed. "I imagine we would have a very well-developed corpse."

The man inside was shaking his head as if he couldn't believe how much stronger he had become in the past twenty minutes.

"Seriously," Glendon said, "what you're suggesting couldn't possibly happen. All our studios are hooked up on closed circuit to a master control system under constant observation. In addition, Dr. Savage, our isotron expert, has been working with electrical muscle stimulators for many years. He's one of the country's leading pioneers in the field."

I made a mental note to check with the county medical association people at the first opportunity to find out if Dr. Savage had been alert enough to maintain his batting average with his customers and hold on to his medical license.

Glendon had ushered me out to a narrow winding path bordered with trees, ground-covering plants and exotic wild flowers. I couldn't name one of them. His hand swept grandly to a steel-shuttered building. "Our Cosmetic Facial Surgery Wing."

Nobody was screaming.

"You do plastic surgery here, too?"

Glendon's voice was almost apologetic. "Well, you know, lifts have become status symbols today."

I knew some of the reasons beyond that. Economic, social or psychological. Competing with younger people for jobs. The divorced who want a new look. The rest who don't like what they see when they look into the old mirror on the wall.

Glendon wasn't far behind me. "Of course it's a panacea for those who cannot face up to the ravages of age."

I touched my chin line gingerly, hoping nothing else had gone wrong this trip.

"But we do reject an awful lot of people who request aesthetic surgery. Up to as high as forty percent. Most of these people want a face redo with the same old psyche. Our aesthetic surgeons must be instant psychiatrists."

We skirted the ultimate vanity wing and Glendon had another in his sights. He threw a heavy door open and suddenly we were in the middle of Africa. Giant plants loomed out of the darkness. Lights twinkled down long quiet corridors. The air was moist and humid. I could pick out vagrant scents of eucalyptus, oil of wintergreen, jasmine, olive oil and tar.

"Our indoor mineral springs and baths," Glendon murmured. "Great therapeutic value. Fantastic."

It didn't smell any better than my gym in Santa Monica, but it looked a whole lot more expensive. Far down the hall I could see white-coated attendants gently prodding figures swathed in sheets. It was too steamy to notice any blue-eyed blondes.

The air was better outside and Glendon shot his cuffs. "I've been saving the best for last," he said smilingly. "My pet project, the Body Contrology section."

He made as if to leap toward the corner building. I held up my hand.

He cooled his motor. "Do you have a question?"

"It's about Miss Clayton. Miss Pamela Clayton."

He looked interested. "Are you a friend of the Claytons?"

"It's kind of sudden," I said. "More like a friend of a friend."

Glendon's sensors worked beautifully and he turned away from his Body Contrology studio as if he suddenly loathed it. "Yes?"

"I understand she had an appointment with your hair stylist here yesterday at ten-thirty, and she canceled it."

"Yes?"

"Well, would you know if she did cancel it? Or perhaps never kept it? Or maybe never had the appointment in the first place?"

Glendon's lips were pursed, but he didn't try to kiss me. "I wouldn't know," he said. "Is this matter of the appointment important?"

"Kind of," I said. I glanced at my watch. "She's been missing for twenty-four hours. I happened to be in the neighborhood and I told Mr. and Mrs. Clayton I'd be glad to check it out for them."

"Of course," Glendon said. He turned his back on me. "Why don't we find out?"

He knew a shorter and quicker way back to the main dome. The tawny-haired gray-eyed girl was still at her desk but alone, with nobody to hustle or excite. Glendon approached her swiftly. "I'd like to look at your appointment book, Miss Hill."

It was large and bound, a loose-leaf affair. She handed it up without a struggle. Glendon flipped the top page over. "Yesterday morning, you said?"

I nodded. "Ten-thirty or thereabouts."

He was shaking his mod curled head. "There must be some mistake. Miss Clayton is not listed for an appointment."

"She wasn't?"

His head wigwagged a few more times slowly. "Besides, ten-thirty wasn't even open. We've a Mr. H. Massin down. He had Mr. K. That's Miss Clayton's usual hairdresser. See for yourself?"

He turned the big book around and my eyes took in both open pages. He wasn't conning me. There wasn't any Miss Clayton on either page and indeed a Mr. H. Massin was down for ten-thirty.

"Thanks," I said. "Sorry to have troubled you."

He gave the book back to the girl. "No trouble. Not at all. I'm sure there's been some kind of misunderstanding. Miss Clayton is probably home by now."

"That's what I told them."

He shrugged negligently. "If it's important to Miss Clayton, I wouldn't care to go on record as contradicting her. You understand."

"Yes."

He smiled and we shook hands and he walked me to the door.

His hand lightly touched the back of my shoulder. "I don't suppose we'll be seeing you again, then, Mr. Roper."

"I wouldn't say that. I like a lot of what I saw here. I might be back sooner than you think."

He bowed. "Good. We'll be looking forward to it."

The big gilded doors closed behind me. I took a deep gulp of the valley air and walked to my car wondering who was kidding whom.

C806046

Six

The sun warmed my back. Horses stomped lazily in their box stalls. A chestnut filly followed me with her eyes and nickered her own come-on. I sucked in my gut and walked on looking for the old man. I found him slumped behind yellow bales of hay in a beat-up captain's chair staring out at nothing.

Cap Abbott was a little older than the hills and looked it. In his day, he'd been the greatest trainer of them all. Horses he had saddled had won three Kentucky Derbies, two Preaknesses and four Belmonts. He had won uncountable millions in purses down the years, had set all-time records for wins during the racing seasons at all the big tracks, owned a triple-crown winner himself. Nevertheless, it was his fashion never to bet more than a deuce on a race.

"Mr. Abbott?" The china-blue eyes fixed on my face and he nodded. "I'd like to talk to you about Willie Rich."

He waved me to an adjacent bale of hay. "Rest your feet, son."

I explained my visit and he listened, his eyes shifting to the track below where a horse was cantering. He eased forward in his chair, folding his hands. His shoulders were bent with the years, his voice gone a shade, too.

There wasn't any warp to his memory. "I celebrated Willie's twenty-first birthday with him right here. It seems a long time ago. He had a consecutive triple that day. Wildside, Up The Creek and Dream Dancer. That Dancer was a nice filly. She paid twenty-nine thirty." He shifted his feet and spat tobacco juice. "Willie didn't change the odds much in those days."

"How's it been lately?"

"Now that's a funny thing, mister. For a long while there a horse with Willie up would drop from a ten-to-one shot and go off a five-to-two. Lately it's been the other way again. He's been on a lot of twelve-to-one types which run like it."

"Any particular reason?"

"Well, Willie was picking his spots this season. He would only ride two or three horses a day when he wasn't busy with other things."

"What other things?"

"Like golf. He was taking a lot of lessons from that old pro Kenevan at La Costa, near Poway." The cold blue eyes that had seen more horses take to their heels than Genghis Khan narrowed. "Last year this time Willie was out in front, but now he was fourth in the ratings. He still was riding some big ones and he got us a winner now and then. Not too bad for a part-time rider."

"Any idea what was on his mind?"

"No. But it was supposed to be on horses and riding. That's all I know."

"Was he depressed enough to kill himself?"

The old boy bristled. "Whatever gave you that notion?"

"Nothing. I can't see Willie taking his own life either."

"Jock takes his life in his hands every day. Several times a day sometimes. But that's a lot different."

"He was only seven wins off Arcaro's stakes record. Don't you think he wanted that one, too?"

Abbott spat in the hay. "Records don't mean a damn thing, son. You break one, there's another one around. The

Princess was Willie's thirty-sixth stakes win this year. Maybe you don't know about another record Bill Hartack rang up one year. Willie was still seven off that one, too."

I had forgotten that one.

"Joey was in the same spot himself, ten years ago."

"Joey?"

Old man Abbott pointed a wavering finger. A little man was coaxing a bay along the rail. "Joey Zale, son. Willie just nipped Joey's old mark on career wins when he took the Princess. But Joey was only six short of Hartack's one-year stakes record when he had his accident."

"What happened?"

"The filly he was riding shied into the rail at the three-eighths pole, shattered her foreleg, and had to be destroyed. That was Want Not, a good three-year-old. The Debutante Stakes."

"What happened to Joey Zale?"

The old gent clicked his store teeth. "He got thrown. You can see what happened to him."

I could see the grotesque limp now.

"Broke his hip, pelvis and back. His leg went in three places. So did his career."

"What does he do now?"

"Grooms horses. Cleans tack. Walks hots. Gallops some workouts."

Stable hand. Exercise boy.

"Tough," I said.

Abbott nodded. "Joey had something none of them had, including Willie. He could talk to horses."

I waited.

"His greatest one-man show, his best year was in forty-eight." The cold blue eyes of the old man flicked back into instant recall. "The season ran fifty days then. They ran eight races daily, not nine. Joey rode the card, all eight races, twelve times. He rode a hundred winners. He had sixty seconds, thirty-three thirds. He was blanked on only three of the forty-six days he rode."

It sounded like one hell of a record.

"Maybe you know. Willie beat it. He came in with five more winners. One oh five. The same number of seconds. Five more for show. Thirty-eight. An in-the-money average of sixty-five point three."

I knew about the sweat and fear that every jock carries in a race. I wondered how Joey Zale felt about Willie Rich passing his mark.

"Willie never mentioned it," I said. "What about Labor Day? Was there any pressure on Willie for the Princess Stakes?"

The octogenarian blinked. "Pressure?"

"Maybe somebody didn't want Calamity to win it."

"I did," Abbott said heavily. "So did Clayton, the owner. I handle some of his horses along with a few of mine and several other owners. What did Calamity pay?"

"Four sixty."

"Not a real big longie. You'd have had to put down a helluva bundle to get rich on that one. It's not easy for a jock to pull a horse, you know. We've got paddock judges, patrol judges and stewards watching with their glasses glued on every race. Complete movies are taken. If a jock does anything wrong, he's set down. If he doesn't follow the orders of the owner and trainer, he's fired. Jocks are like other athletes, too. They have their bad days. They're not hot every time out.

"Sometimes even if the trainer, owner and jock decide the horse is ready, the horse may not feel like competing. Or maybe they forgot to tell him this race was really for the money.

"If that isn't enough, you've still got to talk to all the other jocks and horses in the race, don't you? Maybe you can tell the jocks who you want to win. But it's hard to convince all those other horses that they ought to be taking it easy in the stretch. If they feel like running they just might not believe you."

"I understand Mrs. Clayton had a mare in the race."

"Sister Sally? Sure. Now that was a longie. She didn't race at all the year before last. Last year she ran far back in her three starts. She rated a hundred to one." His head cocked back as he reviewed the past. "I remember some lady betting a hundred dollars on some terrible dog to win. The horse paid two hundred eighty-one dollars and forty cents. That was the only wager on her. The woman took home over fourteen thousand."

I couldn't see Mrs. Tyler Clayton needing fourteen grand.

"Funny thing was," Abbott was saying, "Mrs. Clayton wanted Willie to ride her mare. For sentimental reasons, of course. It was to be Sally's last race. But, of course, Willie was already down for the boss's filly Calamity."

I remembered the stretch run of the old mare. "She came on pretty strong, though, and challenged, didn't she? Maybe she stood a chance, at that."

"She gave it a whirl," the old man said. "But, what the hell, she's been saving it all these years." He winked. "You know how it is when the old gals want their final fling." He hawked and spat again. "Besides, Humble Hilda was the favorite, not Calamity. She hung and Willie went right through on the rail. If you ask me, Mr. Clayton was just being nice to his missus, letting her put her mare in there. On form everybody knew she didn't rate with the others."

A graceful chestnut was cantering around the rail, tossing her head, giving her exercise boy trouble. It looked a lot like the filly who had looked me over on the way in and laughed.

"Damn fool!" Abbott muttered. "What's she doing?"

He shoved himself off his chair and hurried down to the rail. Somewhere along the way he'd picked up a newspaper and now he started waving it, rolled up. The rider sat high forward, urging the gay filly toward the rail, but she wasn't having any of it.

Cap Abbott's face was screwed up. "Oh, well, what the hell. Let her go, dammit. If she wants to go that bad, let her!"

He brought his rolled-up paper down on the rail with a resounding thwack. The filly's eyes rolled and she side-stepped and whistled. Then suddenly her long graceful neck was stretched out and her hooves were hammering into the red turf. The tiny figure of the jock shifted, trying to hold on as they went flying past us and into the turn.

I noticed suddenly the exercise boy had long blond hair and a bright, excited youthful face. When they made the turn, I looked at Abbott. "What kind of an exercise boy is that?"

He grinned. "Cute, huh? It's the new breed. She just sat herself right down on my doorstep and wouldn't move unless I let her ride."

"What's her name?"

"Cynthia Meadows. She's a chem major at UC San Diego, but all she really wants is to be a jock and wear the silk. Can you beat it?"

I shook my head. "For a second there, I thought she might be Clayton's daughter."

Old man Abbott turned and looked at me. "Wish I could help you there, mister, but I don't know any more about that than you do."

The girl who dug horses more than chemistry was letting the filly go and they were flying down the back stretch. They looked great together, but I needed answers more. I thanked the old man and turned to go.

"I liked Willie," he said, his eyes still on the flying filly. "After you've gone up and down the line, and you think you've got something, come on back and we'll talk. Maybe by then, we'll have a clearer picture."

I nodded. "Who owns the chestnut filly, Mr. Abbott? I like the way she runs."

"Oh, that's Mary Jane, Miss Clayton's horse."

"She looks awfully fast. How come she didn't go in the Princess?"

Cap Abbott sighed and pulled out an old corncob. "She never came up with her entry fee, son. Six thousand dollars.

Now, that was Miss Clayton's decision. Maybe after you've asked more of your questions and know some of the answers, you'll have the right one for that, too."

The way things were going, I doubted that. The spirited filly was coming around the far turn now. I decided to get out of there before she finished her run and gave me the horselaugh again. "Just one more question, Mr. Abbott. How did Miss Clayton and Willie's wife get along?"

"They didn't."

Old man Abbott was too old and good a trainer to double in ventriloquism. I turned and looked down into hot yellow eyes. They continued the twisted snarl his face and body carried. "You're Joey Zale?"

"Yeah. What are you—fuzz?"

"No. Private dick. Willie was a friend of mine."

"Too bad it didn't do him any good."

He wore a lot of clothing for a hot day. Sweater, windbreaker and cap. His seamed face had a bluish cast. There were dark pockets under those yellow mocking eyes and his lips were blue. I couldn't tell if he had a heart or kidney problem or if his accident had taken away his circulation along with everything else that mattered. "Can we talk, Joey?"

"Sure." He inclined his head toward the old man. "Cap?"

The old boy waved his hand, his eyes glued to the oncoming filly rushing down the stretch. "Give the man whatever you can, Joey. I've got to ask Miss Chemistry from San Diego why she lets Mary Jane go wide on the turn."

I followed the little gnomelike man as he led the big bay up the incline on a halter. Nearing the stall, he muttered something under his breath and the bay lifted its head and nodded twice and walked into the stall by himself. It could have been habit, and then again maybe Zale could talk to horses at that.

Joey Zale cupped his hands and lit a cigarette, inhaling straight down to his dusty black boots. Most jocks are little men with strong hands, but Zale's were the largest I'd ever seen, with wrists as thick as the average man's ankle. He was thick in the chest and shoulders, too, a good strong middleweight above the waist, and only his legs were pipestem-thin. I could see it didn't matter a bit whether he could talk to horses or not. He had the strength and power where it was needed to handle them and keep them honest and their minds on business, to make those scatterbrained horses listen.

I started with the basic question. "Do you think Willie killed himself?"

"If he did, he coulda done it right here if he wanted. Willie didn't need no pool. He hated water."

"Could he swim?"

"I dunno, but I think it's harder anyway if they hold your head down long enough."

"Who's 'they,' Joey?"

He grinned mockingly at me. "I heard of you, Roper. I know your scene. Christ, if you don't know who the 'they' is, we all got trouble."

I shook my head. "I spoke to Penny, Clayton and Cap Abbott. Nobody knows anything about any heat or pressure for Willie."

"You watched the green board, didn't you?"

"Yes."

"It changes with the odds every ninety seconds, you know. Every dollar changes it."

"I know."

"Any big bet like, say, ten grand or twenty-five G's would scramble the odds the next ninety seconds around and make the tote board change. It could drop any horse six to seven points."

"I know," I repeated. "The board held up."

Joey opened his big gnarled hands. "Then there's your answer, ain't it? The big boys, the betting mob, ain't in it. They didn't have any kind of play going. So it's got to be some different kind of operator had it in for Willie."

"I need a lead to get started, Joey. Anything. Anybody."

He grinned. "You got one already. You don't need no help."

"Penny?"

"I don't think so."

"Clayton's kid?"

"That's it. Only don't ask me why because I don't know."

"Maybe you can tell me if they were close."

"Who?"

"Willie and Pam Clayton."

He flipped his butt into the air and watched it sail toward a tin black water pail. It dropped in neatly. I heard it hiss out. "How's that?" Zale asked. "Close enough?"

Seven

I checked the phone directories but couldn't find any H. Massin listed. I dialed Information and the lady there couldn't help me either. "Do you know what city?" she asked and I had to admit I didn't. "The party might be listed in San Diego or La Jolla," she said. I told her thanks and to forget it. I called the Gilded Cuckoo and asked for Miss Hill at the reception desk. She was out. I asked if they had an address for a Mr. H. Massin and they said they were very sorry but they were not allowed to give out that information and I should check the telephone directories.

I tried a few local bars to find out if anybody knew anything about Willie's whereabouts after the eighth race on Labor Day. Nobody knew a thing. I looked around and asked, but there weren't any blue-eyed blond heiresses reported hung over either. I called the Claytons. The maid answered and told me they were out. She didn't know where. I asked her if Miss Clayton had returned and she said she hadn't. I asked her if she had any idea where she might be and she didn't. I went home.

The telephone was ringing when I got back to my apartment in Santa Monica. It was Allie Riegel. He asked if I knew anything yet. I told him I'd made a lot of tracks and didn't

45

know a damn thing. "There's a chance Willie and Pam meant something to each other," I told him.

"I could have told you that," Allie said.

I let that go. "What do you know about the Gilded Cuckoo?" I asked.

"I love your body the way it is, darling," he said. "Don't change a muscle."

"They saw it as fat."

"Well, they don't know you like I know you."

"Mrs. Clayton," I said. "What do you know about her?"

"A very wealthy woman," he said. "But too old for you."

"Maybe but I wouldn't care to bet on it. She's got something."

"I told you. An awful lot of money."

"Something else, Allie. I got the strangest feeling I know her."

He snickered. "Of course you do."

"Do I?"

"You've seen her in maybe only forty or fifty pictures."

"Movies?"

"Monica Moore was a pretty big star fifteen or twenty years ago. Mostly B pictures. The kind you ate up."

The stagy gestures were still there. "What happened to her movie career?"

"Men, mostly. A lot of booze and maybe some drugs. She had a few bad marriages, or anyway nothing lasted for long."

"How many?"

"Three or four. Maybe five. Who remembers?"

"How long has she been married to Clayton?"

"About a year. But she's straight now. Off the booze. Making a new life. A happy lady living in the country. Horse woman, society and all that jazz."

"Any of her ex-husbands still living?"

"I imagine so. It wasn't that long ago. I remember one owned a string of hotels. The other was a Mr. Universe or something."

"That's all you remember?"

"Say, two out of five isn't bad. I'm paid to do security, not gossip."

"Thanks, Allie. Let me know if you get a lead on the kid."

"Sure thing. You do the same."

I called an agent pal of mine. "Sid, what can you tell me about Monica Moore?"

"Monica Moore? She's too old for you, Roper. You can do better."

"Seriously."

"If it's serious, maybe you better come down and we'll take a look at it."

"Sid," I said.

"I'm serious, too. If you want to know, you better come down to take a look. I've got a file on her. There's a lot to see."

Sid Pinter was an old-time talent and booking agent with offices in Beverly Hills. His receptionist, secretary and factotum was Helen Shane, a tough cookie with green eyes, a still-curvaceous body and a man-hungry heart. She was a former dancer and had been with Sid so long she had forgotten she was hired help. She tapped her intercom button, leaned up close and yelled, "Pinter, stop playing with yourself! Your friend Roper the tough guy is here. What should I do with him?"

"Why ask me?" Pinter's voice replied. "Ask him. Maybe he has some good ideas."

She smoothed her skirt over her flaring hips and looked up at me. "Have you?"

"I wouldn't know one if it walked up and bit me. How are you, Miss Shane."

"Beautiful," she said. "Fantastic. Lovable and seductive. But you don't notice. What's Monica Moore got that I don't?"

"Right now about fifty million dollars and a pregnant mare."

"Jesus!" she said. "I hope to hell you didn't do that!"

Pinter's office wouldn't have won any awards for décor or neatness, but that wasn't his bag. He tapped a thick folder on his desk. In it was a stack of glossy eight-by-tens, publicity stills. Attached to the bottom of each was a small strip of news copy.

Monica Moore, Republic Features starlet, relaxing at Malibu. Photo by World Wide Service.

Tense scene from Monica Moore's latest from Republic Features, Creature from the Dunes, *directed by Irv Pitt. Sam Person, producer.*

She had been a beauty and no mistake. A sinuous figure with eye-popping curves. Classical face, lovely and expressive. Legs that could make a strong man whimper. Lips that pouted or smiled or framed horror and kept your attention, along with the rest of her.

I riffled through. There was Monica Moore wearing very little at the beach, in dungarees barefooted digging for clams, on a fence, up a tree, in a car with at least thirty-five cylinders under its block-long hood. Caught at the premiere of her new feature, *Death Comes at Dawn.* Breaking a bottle over a hull at the Navy yard. Fishing, diving, skiing. Looking demure in gingham and exotic in black lace. Entering Ciro's, the Mocambo, the Trocadero on the arms of smiling men with expensive tans.

Action stills from her various films. In a gorilla's arms, bitten by a vampire, frozen in fear before a shapeless shadow, hand to her throat. (The pose in Tyler Clayton's study that I had somehow curiously remembered.)

I looked at Sid Pinter. "She's been out of pictures for a long time. How come you still have all these photos?"

He shrugged. "Because I'm a saver. A squirrel. I can't throw things away. Some people save coupons, or money, or hard feelings. I save junk. Memories. But if I didn't, you'd be looking around, calling up people, walking your feet off, trying to find out what you want about Monica Moore."

"It was just a question, Sid, not an indictment."

I held another photo. Monica Moore was running down some church steps with a tall laughing fair-haired man. The caption read: *Blushing bride and grinning groom! Monica Moore gets her leading man for keeps! Mr. and Mrs. Jeff Hunter now off for prolonged honeymoon.*

"Jeff Hunter. Who was he?" I asked.

"Number one."

"An actor?"

"Yes. Wealthy family. Owned part of Texas and half of Wyoming."

"Good for Monica Moore."

"Yeah. Keep going. Maybe you'll get them all in order."

"All?"

"The happy bride and grooms."

Pinter impatiently selected several from the pile. "Here is number two. The cowboy star, Rex Lenox. That didn't last too long, either.

"There's number three. The hotel man, Charles Chilton. Very wealthy, very. She got a big bundle from him."

"This number four?" I asked.

"No. I had him someplace. Look for muscles."

He was good-looking, curly-haired, a gleaming torso like Grimek had. It had to be at least a nineteen-inch arm around Monica Moore's waist.

"That's him," Pinter said. "Lance Kite. Former Mr. America and Mr. Universe. That's what it says, right? He was number four." He took the photo from me. "I better put that one away. Miss Shane might see it and start fantasizing."

"I suppose that one didn't last long either?"

"You suppose right. They had a lot of fights, shenanigans in public. She took off, or he took off, I forget which. He got a couple of bit parts in movies because of her name, nothing much. All he really had was his muscle-flexing act."

"What happened to Monica?"

"It was all downhill after that. A lot of bad publicity. She was seen around with the wrong people. She started really hitting the bottle. She had fights with producers and directors. She walked out on a lot of contracts. You'd read about her here and there. Africa, Spain, Morocco, Sarawak. A lot of big shots were still interested in her. She still made an occasional headline. Then, after a while, nothing.

"When she came back after a few years, she found out Hollywood had forgotten her. She tried to make a comeback, but she'd never really been that big a name. She got nowhere. She tried everything and everybody. She even fired her agent."

"Okay, Sid. Now you're going to tell me how it is you have her complete file."

"I saved it for last. Marty Flax, who handled her, was an old friend of mine. She not only fired him, she sued him for mismanagement. He had all this stuff piled up to prove she was losing her own ball game with the fights, jumping contracts. He gave me the complete file before he died, in case she ever looked me up. So I'd know what I was getting into."

I stared at him. Pinter shrugged, found another file and handed it to me. "I see you don't know what I'm talking about. Here's the kind of *tsuris* she was having."

It was his word for trouble. I thumbed through the pile. "Dissolution" would have been as good or better. Her shapely curves were still visible, but could have been supported by an elastic sheath. Her face began to show the booze, the dissipation. The posed publicity still shots by studio cameramen gave way to news photos. She was making all the papers and wire services.

Captions and clipped newspaper columns told the story. *Monica Moore, Republic movie queen, caught in drug raid at beach hideaway.*

Pictures showed her heading for the tank for drunken driving. Abusive language to the arresting officer. Patrolman

Ernie Catropa looked hurt. Others showed her half-dressed, half-crocked. Flying at reporters and photographers like a harridan. *Monica belts movie mag reporter.*

They found her with the racketeers, the old Sunset Strip mob. Night-club scenes. The good old days, the front tables, face-slapping bits, champagne in the eye. Tipsy-toed on the sidewalk. Her beauty was a fugitive thing now. Despair was locked in her eyes.

I turned over the last of it. "This last batch belongs in a newspaper morgue, Sid. Not an agent's files."

He nodded gloomily. "That's what Marty Flax told me when he passed it along. He had it for evidence but never used it at the trial. Everybody knew she was dead in pictures anyway. Then right afterward Marty died."

"When did he die?"

"Right after he won the suit."

"Any particular cause of death?"

Sid tapped his chest.

"Tough, Sid," I said. "Did she try to get you to handle her?"

He shook his head. "She quit show biz. She got into some kind of religion instead."

"Yoga?"

"Not exactly. Not Eastern, not that kind. Something else, some kind of metaphysics. Psychic power. Astral and cosmic magnetism, you should excuse the expression."

"That's a switch," I said.

Pinter scratched his bald head. "I'm trying to think of the guy's name. Charnock, I think. That's him—Louis Charnock. He gave public lectures. Helped you find and put the miracle in your life. That kind of crap."

The name Louis Charnock sounded as if I'd heard it somewhere, but I didn't hear any bells ringing.

"Are you saying Monica Moore joined up with Charnock?"

Pinter stared at me belligerently. "Who said anything like that? It was more like she backed him. He was just coming on, doing the lecture bit. New York, Cleveland, Frisco, here—the big cities, pulling a few nuts here and there, building some kind of following. A lot of people take that stuff seriously, you know."

"Maybe he had something they wanted," I said.

"Sure. That psychic stuff and health and long life appeals to a lot of people, and they're not all kooks either. Anyway, Monica went to a few lectures of his and was bit. I don't know what he gave her, but it seemed to straighten her out. I don't know what she gave him, either. She'd made out pretty heavy in all her settlements, but she must have run through a hell of a lot, too. But they were together a lot, and so far as I know, Charnock never wasted a second on any dame unless she could pay for it. So your guess is as good as mine. She sold her big house and effects around that time, and I think I remember hearing a rumor she was strapped, but that's not hard to figure when you're unloading everything. Anyway, that's all I know and I haven't heard a word about her since —until you mentioned her name."

"Rest your mind, Sid. She's in clover again. She has a new husband with so many millions you'd need a computer to get it all down. Big oil man down Rancho Santa Fe way, Tyler Clayton."

Pinter spread his hands. "That's fine with me. I'm happy for her and glad she made it. She was a beautiful kid with nothing in her head, and they hustled her and crowded her and she didn't know how to handle herself. I don't think she ever really hurt anybody, but they racked her up good and crucified her. The scandal nearly ruined her, right at the beginning."

"Which scandal was that?"

"Didn't I tell you? Her first husband died mysteriously only a few months after they were married. Number one— that was the actor, Jeff Hunter."

"What kind of mysterious circumstances?"

"Sleeping pills. An overdose."

"How about all the others? They still living?"

"So far as I know, yes."

"How about Charnock? He still operating?"

"I think so." He stared silently for a moment at the photos spread out on his desk. "Why not? It's a business with him."

I put out my hand. "Thanks, Sid. I'll see you."

"Don't thank me," he said. "Every time you come to me for some cockamamie information, they jump on you and knock your head in."

"Not this time, Sid. This time it's different."

He looked at me, disbelief written all over his face.

"I don't know who anybody is, Sid, and they don't know me. I'm investigating the death of Willie Rich."

"The jockey? I was reading about it."

"He was a friend, Sid. I think he was murdered."

"Terrible," he said. "The gangsters in that business." He started to put the pictures back into the folder and stopped. "So what does Monica Moore have to do with all this?"

I shook my head. "Nothing really, Sid. Her new husband, Tyler Clayton, happens to own a few thoroughbreds. Race horses. Willie Rich rode one of them Labor Day. Brought him in a winner. Willie died that night. Drowned in his own swimming pool."

Pinter was looking at a half-smoked cigar in his ashtray, as if trying to decide whether to relight it or not. He picked it up and flicked away the ash. "So what are you doing here?"

"I stopped by to ask Mr. Clayton a few questions. He introduced me to his wife, Monica. She looked slightly familiar, but I couldn't pin it down. Then I learned she used to be a movie star going under the name of Monica Moore. That's it, Sid. That's all there was to it."

He rolled the dead cigar in his fingers. "That's all?"

"Almost all. Their daughter—Tyler Clayton's daughter—is missing. Disappeared the same day they ran the Princess Stakes."

"You don't tell me," Pinter murmured.

"I don't know if there's any tie-up or not," I said, and walked to the door. "I'm trying to find out who killed Willie, and why. I'm also trying to locate the girl."

Pinter nodded. "You should only live so long," he said.

Eight

I was nursing a beer in my digs a little later, flipping through the entertainment section of the local sheet, wondering how I was going to kill the evening. I saw his name and sat up straighter.

Charnock.

It was a small ad tucked between the various movie houses.

CHARNOCK
presents
"The Cosmic Miracle"
Learn to attract and
Magnetize what you want
in Life.

A public lecture. Tonight at 8 P.M. Wilshire Park Playhouse.

I was there early. The Wilshire Park Playhouse was an esoteric showcase for the dance, for small operettas, for public lectures and demonstrations. It was down past the old Miracle Mile, a slightly down-at-the-heels but still respectable neighborhood. It held fifteen hundred seats, and I could tell most of them were going to be filled this evening.

His picture braced you from a large easel in the lobby. He looked too young and handsome still and it had to be an old photo. Clear eyes stared limpidly and without guile into mine. He looked clean-cut and vibrant, not a bad sort, but then a lot of con men look that way, and it's all in their favor. Some are even good guys at heart, but they like to sell themselves and they like to influence people, and they like the long lines and the clink of coins at the box office. It doesn't matter much what they're selling. Somehow they have the power to magnetize a lot of foolish people into doing foolish things.

Another easel on display listed the evening's contribution from Charnock: *How to focalize your cosmic perception. Project your thoughts into the gold of health, happiness, love and illimitable treasures.*

There wasn't any price listed for this psychic unfoldment. That meant voluntary contributions, and a lot of people are unable to get up and out in time and find it difficult to resist putting a little something into the donation basket when it's passed down the aisles.

A linen-covered table against the wall presided over by some silver-haired old ladies was covered with books, pamphlets and small dishes for coins. There were various booklets for Charnock's course. *The Occult Law of Mental Alchemy. Astral Ascent to Mystic Realms. How to Develop Your Cosmic Perception.* Tuition was listed at twenty dollars and there were dates and times for the classes to begin.

The incoming crowd was orderly and soft-spoken, middle-aged mostly, some elderly couples. As they straggled into the lobby they headed directly for the tables where Charnock's books were on sale. The silver-haired ladies didn't high-pressure anybody or hustle them into buying, and they had all they could do to keep up with sales. Charnock's books, I noticed, were all on his favorite subjects, cosmic magnetism, the magic power of the occult law, miracles of cosmic perception, and how to use any or all of these for long life, happiness and untold wealth. Most of the ladies picked up a book or a pamphlet, their escorts deferring to their spouses' greater needs, and then they filed into the theater and found seats and waited for the man to appear who had found a shortcut to Nirvana.

I took a seat halfway down at the side. There were soft murmurs of excitement and expectancy as the lights dimmed. A chunky broad-shouldered man dressed all in white came out of the wings and sat down at an organ. He pressed his pedals and released some hymnlike sonorous chords and progressions. Then the spotlight came on, centering its circle, and when it was fixed a man strode briskly out from the wings, nodded to the man at the organ, stopped at the center of the spotlight, and began to speak. Like his accompanist at the organ, he too was in white.

He wasn't that young or handsome any more, and I pegged his age near the fifties even with the make-up. His eyes were dark and intense, his gestures few and limited, but his voice was mellifluous, the voice of a dramatic actor who knew how to use it. He didn't waste a word. That was where the money was.

His style was neighborly with homespun philosophy. The organist had pealed his last chord and Charnock now made his own music, his voice rising and falling dramatically with convincing sincerity. He spoke about our human need for love, happiness, peace of mind, the attainment of wealth, and he hinted at the inner illumination we all had within ourselves waiting to be released, and how he would give us the key.

The large audience was still and attentive, hanging raptly on every clearly enunciated syllable. The houselights were on dimly, and they sat with folded hands, transfixed by Charnock's soothing cadence. I looked around and I could see every eye upon him, glistening with attention, as they smiled and nodded.

A door opened at the rear of the theater. There was a

rustle and the faint muffled sound of footsteps coming down the aisle. A latecomer had been admitted and a few disturbed souls, their concentration broken, glanced around annoyed. It was a woman, and she found a seat empty on the aisle and slipped into it quietly. Charnock's voice rose and they forgot all about her and returned their attention to him.

I didn't. I sat, curious and surprised, wondering why Mrs. Monica Clayton was here. It was a long trip to make for a Louis Charnock public lecture, a long ride from Rancho Santa Fe. I wondered why, after all the years, having it made now, rich and secure at last, she still needed to hear the master's voice.

I didn't get it and because it bothered me, I missed learning how to get added power, magnetism and success. I also blew how to make my cosmic miracle happen. Charnock cleverly held this secret revelation as his ace for last, declaring a sudden intermission first. The lights went on and an army of ushers appeared in the aisles. There was a donation basket for each row, to be passed along, contributions voluntary. One came my way loaded with bills, and I quickly passed it on to my immediate neighbor. I was already illuminated with Charnock's theory about the attainment of wealth, and we only differed as to who was to get it. I managed to beat a few other unregenerate cheapskates to the sidewalk, but not all.

I waited and a little later the crowd spilled out. I watched for Monica Clayton, but she didn't show. The chunky white-suited organist came out and went to one of the tables and helped sell some of Charnock's books. Then Charnock appeared, looking tired and a little older. A gaggle of women clung to his coattails, bought his books, and begged for his autograph, but Monica Clayton wasn't among them. Charnock shook hands, signed, thanked his following, and let the chunky man handle all the money. After a while, he begged off and walked around the corner. A big black limousine was parked at the curb. A burly tough-looking driver sat behind the wheel. As Charnock stepped in, a shadowy figure on the rear seat moved. The car moved off slowly and the streetlight revealed Monica Clayton's pale face. She sat stiffly, not smiling.

Charnock appeared not to notice.

Nine

The long Labor Day holiday weekend was over. I hadn't made a dent in my investigation of Willie Rich's strange death by an overdose of water from his swimming pool. I didn't know any more about Tyler Clayton's missing daughter than I knew before. I had unlocked a considerable bit about Mrs. Clayton's past as Monica Moore, and had accidentally stumbled upon a mysterious evening rendezvous between her and Louis Charnock. It wasn't much. Given her background for being disaster prone, I could only assume she was off again on another tangent, if indeed she had ever been safely grounded. They could have been old friends getting together again, for all I knew, at another time of crisis in her life, her husband's daughter missing and his favorite jockey killed. Maybe Charnock, for all his two-bit metaphysical mouthings, knew the answers to keeping her sane and healthy under stress. According to my friend Sid Pinter, she had already been pilloried and brutalized enough. There was no need for me to get heavy and lean on her.

I went down to the EPT offices on Wilshire to go to work.

EPT means Emergency Procedure Terminus. It stands for big troubles and the solutions thereof. O. J. Burr runs the place, his own private cloak-and-dagger intelligence operation. He has a hand-picked staff of capable investigators who work very closely under his direction. We've fronted for a lot of gung-ho government operations which need our kind of cover, assisted police authorities with murders and kidnappings, nark agents with dope rings, and even helped the average citizen if he was wealthy enough or if O. J. became interested in his particular problem.

When Allie Riegel called me in on Willie's death, he hadn't specified the kind of power investigation EPT might do. It was strictly between me and him. You do for friends.

There were no renegade spies on the morning roster for me to deal with, nobody muscling in on the Women's Lib group, and all the agitation at the local institutions of learning had somehow been contained for the moment. I hate to take good money from O. J. for sitting around and doing nothing but look and lust at our inordinately beautiful secretarial go-between, Miss Troy. It would be more rewarding if Miss Troy knew I was alive, but somehow, despite her efficiency, I'm merely the desk for the incoming mail or the phone extension for O. J. Burr.

He rang, wanted to know what I had been doing, and I told him. "That's all you've accomplished?" he asked, surprised.

"I'm disappointed, too," I said. "I can't seem to get rolling on anything."

"Willie Rich was a friend of yours?"

"Yes."

"Then what are you doing here? I'll get in touch with you if we need your services."

"Thanks, O. J.—but—"

"I'll give you a week. Wrap it up."

I went downtown to the LAPD Headquarters and asked for Captain Scott, who ran the Bunco and Forgery Division. He didn't keep me waiting and I didn't waste his time either.

"Charnock?" he repeated. "Louis Charnock?"

"I was hoping you'd have heard of his operation. Maybe

he's been defrauding widows of their life savings. Taken a lot of those little old ladies from Pasadena in tennis shoes."

He picked up a phone and growled into the mouthpiece. A few minutes later a pretty young thing in a short skirt masquerading as a policewoman came into his office. She dropped a thick folder on his desk and left without asking if there was anything else.

"What was that?" I asked.

"Something they threw in to make the job tougher," Scott muttered.

I shook my head and clucked sympathetically. It was good to know our Miss Troy wasn't the only distraction and crimp in the wheel of good solid concentrated investigative effort.

Scott threw the file open and thumbed through several pages. "Just wanted to refresh my memory. There's nothing new on him. Do you have a complaint?"

"No. Not yet anyway. I heard a little about him and caught his act last night. I wondered what you might have."

"Nothing much. We've had an eye on him for twenty years. There have been a few complaints, but nothing we could hit him with and make stick. You know this town. It's always gone for the quacks and saviors."

"What kind of complaints?" I asked.

"Then, again," Scott continued, "you'd be surprised at how many people swear by him. That he's given them inspiration and reason for living."

"I'm sure he has. What kind of complaints?"

"Standard. He gets a good play with donations. That's a willful contribution. Nothing coercive about that. Strictly legal."

"Who's complaining?"

"Well, you know if you've seen him that he gets the women. They can't wait to put money into his hands. Sometimes their husbands don't cotton to that kind of generosity."

"Anything else?"

"He's broken up a few homes. Sometimes a few of them

forget they've got husbands, kids, families—and dump everything to follow him around. But he's very careful, and his main game is the widows, especially the wealthy ones. You'd be surprised how many of them turn over their annuities to him. Remember him generously in their wills. Holdings, estates, businesses. Again, it's of their own free will. Nobody's put a gun to anybody's head."

"Never? In all these years? He calls himself a philosopher. He's bound to have made a mistake somewhere along the line."

Scott nodded and grinned crookedly. "He's been careful all along. There's another man in his operation. Dorn."

"Dorn?"

"Wesley Dorn. He works with Charnock. Plans the bookings and takes care of the travel and reservations. Helps distribute and publish Charnock's books. Does publicity and promotion. Greets the little old ladies. Plays the organ background music."

I remembered the chunky unobtrusive broad-shouldered man. "What about Dorn?"

Scott shrugged and threw his hands apart. "He handles the money end of it. Keeps Charnock always in the clear."

I don't care how smart they are. They all have to make the blunder at least one time. It's statistical. "Always?"

Captain Scott scowled down at the file on Charnock. "Well, no. Not always. We nearly had him nailed seven years ago."

"Dorn or Charnock?"

Scott shrugged. "It doesn't matter. I see it as Charnock's operation. Dorn merely fronts for him to keep his name clear."

"What was the complaint?"

"Fellow claimed Charnock broke up his marriage."

I nodded glumly. "As you were saying—standard."

"This fellow's complaint went further. He claimed a five one nine."

"Extortion?"

"Yes. You're familiar with the four parts of the section?"

I knew them well enough. Under California law, fear, such as will constitute extortion, may be induced by a threat:

1. To do an unlawful injury to the person or property of the individual threatened or of a third person; or,

2. To accuse the individual threatened, or any relative of his, or member of his family, of any crime; or,

3. To expose, or impute to him or them any deformity, disgrace or crime; or,

4. To expose any secret affecting him or them.

Section 519 is punishable by imprisonment in the county jail not longer than one year or in the state prison not exceeding five years, or by fine not exceeding five thousand dollars, or by both such fine and imprisonment.

I admitted I knew the section.

Scott turned the page. "He charged Charnock with extortion, but his wife refused to sign the complaint. He then claimed the sums she had paid Charnock constituted part of his rightful property under California community property law."

"Sounds more like a civil action," I said. "Did he get half his money back?"

Scott smiled. "That was another point. It was his wife's money. Her income. He wasn't working."

"Still—"

"He was persuaded somehow to withdraw his complaint. It never came to trial. Apparently they settled out of court."

"Did he ever get his wife back?"

"No."

I took out my little notebook. "What was his name? Perhaps he might be able to give me some more information."

"Lance Kite."

"Number four," I said.

Scott stared, puzzled. "Number four?"

"He wasn't the first for Monica Moore." I recited them in the sequence Sid Pinter had given me. "Jeff Hunter, an actor, was number one, her first. Then Rex Lenox, the cowboy. A hotel man, Chilton, was number three. The muscleman was number four—Kite."

Scott closed the folder and lit his pipe. "Maybe you won't mind telling me why you're here wasting my time with questions when you know as much or more about it than I do."

"Fair enough," I said. "But I didn't know that much when I came in here. Let me have Kite's last address before you put that thing away, and I'll fill you in."

He gave it to me, I wrote it down, and I started with the call from Willie Rich the night before the Princess Stakes at Del Mar on Labor Day.

He heard me through and shook his head. "That isn't our office and I'd have to check with homicide, but to my knowledge Willie's death is down as accidental death by drowning."

"I'm trying to prove otherwise," I said. "Also, Monica Moore is now Mrs. Tyler Clayton, down in old Rancho Santa Fe. That makes *him* number five, you see."

Scott's eyebrows lifted. "It might make him number ten, for all you or I know. Who's the official scorer?"

"Maybe her conscience. Apart from my not being a fan of Louis Charnock's, I've another problem."

Scott didn't shut the door in my face and I told him about Pam Clayton, the missing heiress. "That's a problem, all right," he said. "And, fortunately, yours, not mine. Is she over eighteen?"

"Yes."

"You call that a problem?" Scott demanded. "Kids are disappearing, running away from home, all over the country, and a lot of them are under fourteen."

"I know," I said. "That's another problem. Regarding Miss Clayton, so far as her parents are concerned, there is no official statement as to whether she is actually missing or not."

Scott grinned mockingly. "Rotsa ruck," he said.

"Unofficially, Captain," I said, "I'd appreciate it if you got in touch with me in case anything turns up on her."

"I'd be glad to," he said, "but that's not our department. Maybe Missing Persons can help you. Although there's not much chance of that either if her father doesn't ask for police help."

"I realize that."

"The FBI's supposed to be pretty good at that kind of action."

"I know."

Scott looked steadily at me. "I thought you were, too, Roper."

I rubbed my jaw.

"Is the kid pretty?" he asked.

"Very," I said. "Extremely. Judge for yourself."

I showed him the picture I had of Pam Clayton and he nodded several times. "A girl that pretty ought to be right up your alley," he said finally. "Shouldn't take you more than a few days."

"That's what I've been hearing," I said. "Maybe I've been missing something. What makes it so damn easy?"

"Incentive," he said. "You've got incentive."

Ten

The apartment house Lance Kite lived in wasn't the address he had given the Bunco Squad. It was listed in the directory, a comedown from the address he had shared with Monica Moore. A ratty section of West Los Angeles with a good view of the city storm drain. Whatever her settlement out of court had been, apparently it had been no windfall.

He answered the door on the third ring, and although I had seen his picture and knew he was a former Mr. America and ex-Mr. Universe, I was still surprised by his bulk.

There are two extreme kinds of dedicated health and strength nuts, the muscle builders and the weight lifters. The latter don't have to be anything but strong. The muscle builders program themselves differently. They don't care as much about piling on the iron to see how much they can jerk, lift or press. Their interest is mainly in molding their bodies so that every muscle is worked to the limit with the development they want on it. They're as dedicated as the weight men, and work out as hard, but theirs is a different kind of narcissism and ego.

Muscle builders are the pretty boys, the ones you see at the beach flexing their muscles, stretching their lats to impress the little bronzed bunnies who gaze up at them adoringly. If they look good enough and can get a sectional title or two or the big national or international Kite had won, they're apt to get a crack at a flick now and then where the background calls for gleaming well-muscled torsos. The emperor's guard, the pasha's eunuchs. Gladiators for all the revivals of the old Roman scene and the Hercules myth.

The muscular padding is real. Some of them build up so much weight and muscle to match or beat the competition that they build up strength and power, too. To make it as a Mr. America or Universe, you've got to have pushed and pulled more iron than all the other guys sweating it out in gyms throughout the country.

At one time Lance Kite had been the best, and that takes in a lot of other exceptionally developed men. But his best was maybe fifteen years behind him. Life had got at him, and booze. I could see it in his face and smell beer on his breath and it was early in the day. He was still big, and formidable-looking, but he was soft and flabby now, maybe ten or twenty pounds over his best. He was about my height, but he needed a shave more, his eyes were redder, and he wasn't nearly as cheerful.

He stood in the open doorway, glowering at the interruption, trying to knock me over with his breath. He wasn't a bad-looking guy despite a long angular chin, but I wasn't there to make love to him.

"Lance Kite?" I asked pleasantly.

"What about it?"

"Mind if I ask you a few questions?"

"What about?"

"It's private business. Can we talk inside?"

"What the hell for? What's on your mind, pal?"

"I'm trying to get some information about a man called Louis Charnock. I believe you knew him, or of him, once."

His eyes glowered redder and his voice became surlier. "You got his name. Why don't you ask him?"

"You were first on my list," I said. "I got your name from a complaint you once registered with the Bunco Squad."

"Oh, yeah?"

"You were married to Monica Moore at that time."

"What about it?"

"You were her fourth husband?"

He looked down at his hands. "I suppose. So what?"

"I understand she left you for Charnock."

He stared at me and I could see more of the fifty-inch chest under the expanding T-shirt. He didn't answer, and breathed out more beer fumes instead.

"I'd like to find out if he's on the level or running a racket. Your complaint against him was for extortion. It was a long time ago. Maybe you wouldn't mind talking about it."

Kite's lips twisted. "Why the hell should I? Who the hell are you and what's it any of your business?"

"My name's Roper. I'm a private investigator, interested in how Charnock operates. Maybe he can still be nailed. You wouldn't mind that, would you?"

He shifted his feet. "I'd have to think about it."

"Okay," I said. "No hurry. I heard you dropped your complaint suddenly. Mind telling me why?"

"Sure. It's none of your goddam business. That good enough?"

"Fine," I said. "First-rate. Thanks for your time."

I turned to go and he looked surprised. "Hold it," he said. "Did Monica send you?"

I lifted an eyebrow. "Monica?"

"No, huh? But you've seen her around."

I nodded. "Yes."

He hesitated, his eyes shifting past my shoulder. He gave me a little smile. "Maybe you'll see her again. Maybe you can give her a message from me?"

I shrugged. "Maybe."

He nodded, swung the door open a bit, and shifted his feet. "Give her—this!" he said, grinning broadly.

It wasn't much, a heavily muscled twenty-inch arm that he launched from deep in his living room in a long sweeping arc at my chin. It didn't tear my head off because I had already observed all the signs as he prepared for it. My old judo and karate instructor in Japan, the very elderly but expert Professor Takahashi Hamakichi, Eight-Dan, had prepared me well for such chance encounters in life, painfully but memorably.

I moved my head to the right and used left-forefist upper block (*seiken jodan-uke*), revolving my blocking arm in a short counter arc which the old man preferred to the straight line. Inverted-fist strike to the spleen (*uraken hizo-uchi*) was indicated next and I struck swiftly sideways. Kite sagged and retched. I got all the beer fumes he had been saving up. He was set up perfectly for rising-elbow strike (*hiji age-uchi*), but I was fascinated by his long vulnerable jaw and I tagged him on it to find out if it was glass. It was, and Kite sat down with a look of hurt surprise.

I took out my business card and dropped it under his gasping open mouth. "Drop around to see me some time when you feel better. Maybe we can talk some more."

He goggled up at me dazedly. I turned at a sound across the way. A woman had come out her front door. She stood staring now, shaking her head. "You dropped Mr. America? I don't believe it. What'd you hit him with?"

"Incentive," I told her.

Eleven

I phoned the box office of the Wilshire Park Playhouse. The attendant hesitated when I asked where Mr. Charnock was living while in town. I explained it was an urgent matter. It concerned a large donation to his cause. I got the address.

The Regency Arms was a good apartment hotel off Wilshire along the old Miracle Mile. The lobby desk clerk told me Charnock had the penthouse. A small self-service elevator worked its way up to the top. The hall was clean and plush. Red carpet piling over white tile. Green potted plants that had been watered. The suite had double doors. I knocked on one.

A big burly man filled the door opening. His hair was close-cropped, yellow. His eyes were a pale bleached-out blue. He had a flat dented nose, scar tissue over his eyes and ears, and could have been an ex-pug, wrestler or bouncer. He looked like the man behind the limousine wheel the night Monica Clayton had joined Charnock in the car after his lecture.

I wasn't in disguise, but I was playing a part. I cleared my throat and tried to sound impressive and businesslike. If my role convinced Charnock, I'd have a line on him. "Mr. Charnock, please."

He looked me over, glanced at the black attaché case in my hand, and wasn't impressed. "What's it about?"

I handed him a business card. It read: Anthony Hale. Attorney at Law.

Charnock's part-time chauffeur who apparently doubled as bodyguard and bouncer took it between two fingers no thicker than a fungo stick. "You got an appointment?"

I shook my head. "It's about the donation. Mrs. Casper may have called. It concerns her estate and its disposal, you see."

"Wait here. I'll see."

He walked across the sitting room to a closed door at the far end, knocked and entered, closing the door behind him. The room was large, light and well furnished. A stack of Charnock's books and pamphlets covered a table and part of a small sofa. A life-size cardboard replica of Charnock leaned against a wall, apparently a lobby display. Under it in large type was lettered: UNVEILED MYSTERIES OF THE COSMOS.

CHARNOCK
Philosopher of the 20th Century
presents
Class Lessons in Cosmic Metaphysics
Learn to affirm your purposes positively!

The window opposite offered a good view of the street fourteen floors below. There were pictures and a mirror on the wall of the connecting suite opposite, flowers on a stand, a stack of mail already stamped waiting for postal delivery, a batch of two-sheeted throwaway promotion listing the chain of miracles he helped make happen.

I picked one up. The cover showed his picture, staring out with a confident smile, the way he must have looked twenty years before. Running down the other part of the page were several of the miracles spelled out: *Magnetize what you want. Create your own Good Luck. Add Psychic*

Power to enhance your future. Cosmic thoughts as aids to long life and health. The secrets of astral and cosmic powers. The rest of the top page advertised his new book: *Cosmic Reality or Chaos.*

The back of the top page listed his various class lessons, giving specific times and dates, the address and fees. The foldover second page listed Charnock's various popular affirmations, which included peace of mind, money, love, happiness and power.

On the back of the sheet was a short biography of Charnock, covering his background as lecturer, author and philosopher for the past twenty years. A paragraph under that mentioned various movie stars in Hollywood who had been helped in their careers by the methods of Charnock. I glanced over the list of stars, and found one I still remembered. Monica Moore. I folded it and put it in my inside jacket pocket.

The door at the far end opened and the big boy came out. "He's kinda busy but he says he can give you a coupla minutes."

Charnock rose from behind a desk littered with letters, books, pamphlets, pictures and dollar bills. He pushed these aside toward a switchboard panel between an intercom and two telephones. He was wearing his white outfit and black tie. His hand was cool and soft, his voice a gracious deep-throated purr. "Mr. Hale? It is difficult for me to see people without an appointment. Our time is limited and there are so many in need—"

"I understand. But I had to go to court unexpectedly and I had other business in this neighborhood. And then, the matter of Mrs. Casper's estate concerns you, Mr. Charnock."

His face was pockmarked up close, his dark eyes deep-set and penetrating. He looked puzzled and I couldn't blame him. "I'm sorry, but I know nothing about a Mrs. Casper or her estate."

I took the chair opposite him, snapping open my attaché

case. "You may not know her by that name. But you would recognize her easily. She happens to be one of your most ardent followers."

He looked more puzzled still. "Then I don't understand—"

"I'm sorry I am not permitted to reveal more at this time without violating my client's trust," I said. "This matter of her will is a sensitive one. When you and I have completed the preliminaries, you'll understand better the need for the utmost care and discretion."

He blinked. "Well, yes, of course."

I half turned to the big man behind me at the door. "I'm afraid I must be assured of complete privacy from this point on. We can take no risks of a third party being privy to this matter."

Charnock nodded to the man at the door. "Wait outside."

The door closed softly behind me.

Charnock glanced at his watch. "This is all very confusing. You say your Mrs. Casper has come to our lectures?"

"Many times."

"Along with you, sir?"

I shook my head with sincere regret. "Sorry, I haven't yet had the pleasure. The pressure of business. Perhaps I can still make it one night before long—"

His dark eyes probed mine intently, making me wonder briefly if he was putting some of that cosmic psychic magnetism to work. "Our visit will unfortunately be short this time. We have other engagements farther north. Our stay will be two weeks more at the most. We do a week of lectures and follow with two weeks of lessons. Perhaps you will find the time. I can assure you it will be a most profitable evening. Many people quite well known now have benefited."

"So I've heard." I tapped my inner pocket. "I picked up one of your pamphlets inside. Quite an imposing list. I had no idea you've helped so many Hollywood movie stars."

He shrugged negligently. "We merely teach. Those who will, listen. The elements of the Universe are attainable for all. My work is merely transmitting the secret."

His deep resonant voice vibrated with conviction and sincerity. I restrained a wild momentary impulse to give him a million dollars for one good Universal secret.

"You've certainly helped Mrs. Casper, just as you helped the person who recommended you to her." I bit my lip and looked vague. "Sorry, but her name eludes me."

Charnock permitted a trace of levity to slip in. "As does your Mrs. Casper me, I'm afraid."

I smiled. "She's a very cautious woman. She's never given you her correct name."

Charnock folded his hands and tapped his thumbs together. "That's what troubles me. This element of caution you stress so. Perhaps you'd better explain it all."

"Very well. Quite bluntly, Mrs. Casper does not have long to live. She has heirs who are now awaiting her end with impatience rather than sorrow."

"How unfortunate. But you must remember, the will of the Almighty is inscrutable. One can never say for certain when we shall have completed our duties here on earth."

"My feelings, exactly," I said. "But Mrs. Casper's doctors say otherwise. That her death is not only predictable but imminent."

"I see."

"Her condition has suddenly taken a drastic turn for the worse. Hence her immediate concern with my seeing you to work out a sort of conditional arrangement."

He sat back. "Conditional?"

"Yes. The donation or bequest must be anonymous. Absolutely no mention of her name. The heirs might not welcome this dispersal of an estate they somehow conceive of as legitimately part of their rightful inheritance."

Charnock nodded. "You and Mrs. Casper would know their legal situation far better than I, sir."

"Yes, and this matter presents no particular problem in

any respect save that of publicity. You see, there was a good deal of notoriety with that other woman—" I rubbed my scalp for instant recall and found it at last. "—I have it now —Monica Moore. The former movie star. That matter of her husband contesting the disposal of her estate. Do you remember? Apparently it was in all the papers."

His eyes hooded. There was a slight humming sound. One of the lights on his intercom panel glowed red. Charnock rocked back slowly, his fingers tapping at his temple. His eyes closed. "One moment, please," he said softly. "Our cosmic thoughts are not in tune. Let me concentrate a moment."

I watched him concentrate, breathing deeply, sitting back in his chair. The air became close suddenly and I felt the disrupting presence of danger.

"This is a difficult matter," he said finally, his eyes still closed. "I believe it is out of my province. Perhaps you should speak to my associate, Mr. Dorn."

"Fine," I said briskly. "Does he handle the business end of things?"

A harsh voice filtered through a speaker. "Don't bother, Louis. It's a waste of time. The gentleman will be leaving."

The door opened behind me. The big bodyguard stood there with a heavy automatic trained on my midsection.

I looked at Charnock, mustering all my pseudolegal front. "What's the meaning of this? Is that man in your employ threatening me, sir?"

Charnock's lips were pale and parted. He looked ill.

Another man entered briskly. He was chunky and broad-shouldered, wearing a business suit and light-rimmed glasses which glittered. I recognized him as the man who had played the organ the night of the lecture, and greeted the little old ladies afterward, and helped sell them books. He held the business card I had given when I arrived, and stepped up to me quickly out of the line of fire. "It says Anthony Hale on this card. There must be some mistake apparently. It *is* Roper, isn't it?"

"Roper?" I repeated, surprised. "Whatever gave you that idea?"

"The cosmic mind," he said dryly. "Have you forgotten we specialize in attaining the secret powers of the Universe?"

I got up and started to close the snaps of the attaché case on my knee.

He shook his head, half smiling. "One moment, please, Mr. Roper."

The gun was still on me and I let him have the case. He opened it and nodded, satisfied, as he lifted out the small tape recorder I had craftily brought along. "Most ingenious of you," he said. Then he switched the On button to Rewind and spun the tape, wiping out Anthony Hale and his juristic comedy of errors, spun it clean and shut it off.

"I'm advising Mrs. Casper forthwith," I said, "to reconsider. I'm certain she can find other charities eminently more suitable for her considerable fortune."

"I'm sure she can. Show the man out, Jay Jay."

I turned and walked through the door, the big gunsel two-stepping behind me. As he closed the door, I heard Dorn say, "Louis, you're a fool!" followed by some unprintable words.

Immediately there was a slapping sound and a low exclamation of pain. The gun prodded my back.

"Move it, pal."

We made a cozy twosome going out and down the hall to the elevator. He gestured to the elevator button and I jabbed it. The car came up, the door opened, and he watched me walk in. He grinned, saluting me with his upraised gun. "See ya around, pal. Maybe next time we'll both have better luck."

I nodded unhappily and the door closed, dropping secret agent to the bottom of the building slower than he deserved.

You win one. You lose one.

Twelve

I went home and called Allie Riegel down at Del Mar race track. I had to find out if Clayton's daughter had come home yet. There still was a chance her disappearance was coincidental with Willie's death, based on a whim or impulse or whatever it was these days that drove kids. I wanted to get her out of my hair so I could concentrate completely on Willie's case. I couldn't escape the conclusion that if it were anything really serious her old man would take some action. With his name and millions, Clayton had enough clout to make any law-enforcing body jump. But it was still only a couple of days, and I figured maybe she'd done it to him before and this time he'd give her a week before sending out the legal bloodhounds in force. Putting me on it was just a gesture and we both knew it.

Digging up the dirt on Monica Clayton wasn't what I had intended either. Whatever her relationship with Charnock was, it wasn't any of my business. I didn't doubt but there was a lot of unexplained muck in her life I'd come across if I didn't lay off. Some of it might hurt her in her new life with Tyler Clayton. As I saw it, that wasn't my job either, but I kept getting nudged off line.

The extortion complaint from her former husband Lance Kite had seemed sensible enough to check further. If Charnock was a blackmailer, it was conceivable Clayton might be a likely prospect soon, if not already. I wasn't naïve enough not to consider that angle seriously, and their continuing association cast a hell of a shadow on what I saw. It was possible, too, that the missing girl was somehow wrapped up in some plan they had. Although it seemed too obvious and amateurishly suicidal, it couldn't be completely disregarded. Again I figured Clayton certainly had to know something about her past. To my knowledge, owning most of the available currency of the realm doesn't necessarily preclude making damn sure you hold on to it. I assumed he had her checked and double-checked before taking her on as a legal partner in marriage. Considering Clayton's track record in the financial field, I couldn't help but see him as more than a match for any two-bit blackmailing racket. Tycoons like Tyler Clayton simply don't bluff easily. They can always go outside the law if they have to, and take care of their own. Blackmailers can only threaten. The big men of business are geared to being ruthless. Killing somebody in their way, a threat to them, isn't any more difficult than picking up the telephone.

Allie Riegel had picked up his now and was barking hello. I asked him if there was any news of the missing heiress.

"She's still to be regarded as missing," he said, "unless you've managed to find her."

"I haven't had that pleasure. They told me at the Gilded Cuckoo she never kept her appointment Monday morning. She didn't have one. They could could be lying, of course."

"Why would they?"

"I don't know. They've got a lot of space where she could be hiding out, if she wanted to pay the tab."

"You didn't tell me yet why she'd be wanting to hide out."

"I haven't figured that either," I said. "But it's some kind of possibility. Is that place legit?"

"So far as I know it's been around for years and there

hasn't been a rap on it yet. You want me to get the sheriff's office to look it over?"

"No. That would be Clayton's move, if he ever got worried. I'm on it because I don't make waves."

"You don't make much sense either. Have you got anything yet on Willie?"

"Not a whistle. I saw Abbott and Joey Zale. Zale could have a motive if he didn't like the idea of Willie taking up on his last remaining record."

"Are you serious?"

"I'm not sure. You think that's too way-out?"

"How the hell do I know? You're the detective."

"Yeah. Anything new there that you could tell me?"

"Well, Penny has complained that their house has been broken into and ransacked again."

"Again? When did it happen before?"

"A few nights before Willie was knocked off."

"She didn't mention it. Neither did you."

"I just found it out myself. She didn't think it worth mentioning before, as long as Willie didn't seem worried."

"And he wasn't?"

"He never let on to me."

"Has anything been taken from their house?"

"She says, to her knowledge, no."

"That's very interesting," I said.

"Hurry up and tell me why. I've got work to do here."

"It sounds like Willie had something that somebody wanted, still wants. If he knew about it and didn't let on, then he had his hand and was sitting tight. Maybe we finally have something, Allie. Motive."

"Sounds good," he said. "Any idea what it could be?"

"No."

"Let me know when you do," he said. "I've got a real emergency on my hands now I have to take care of."

"Anything I can do to help?"

"Have you lost a little three-year-old boy?"

I hung up. I wondered if the ransacking of Willie's house had been behind his calling me and setting up our get-together. It was a new element to consider. I thought about that, and suddenly I thought about something else I should have thought about and hadn't.

I checked the number and called the Gilded Cuckoo. Her voice sounded fresh and young and familiar.

"Hello, is this Miss Hill?"

"Yes. Who's this?"

"I spoke to you the other day. Did you tell me you were new on the job?"

She laughed. "Not exactly. Only at the reception desk. I was transferred from therapy."

"Then you weren't at the reception desk Labor Day?"

"No. That was Bonnie. I took over the following day."

"Bonnie?"

"Bonnie Burns. She's the regular receptionist."

"Is she there now? Could I speak to her?"

"Sorry, sir. She just went on vacation. She left Monday afternoon."

"Do you have any idea where I could reach her? It's very important."

"You're lucky. We got a post card from her this morning. Wait till I find it." There was silence from her and I could hear drawers opening and closing before she came on again. "She's up in Tahoe. The Totem Lodge."

"Thank you."

"Do you want the phone number? It's right on the picture card."

I called the Lake Tahoe number and asked for Bonnie Burns.

"She's not staying at the main lodge. She has one of the cabins along the lake. I'll try her there. That's cabin number five."

She came on in a few minutes, cheerful and curious. "Bonnie speaking. Say, who *is* this?"

I told her.

"Are you sure you have the right number? I don't need a detective."

"I've a few questions, Miss Burns. They won't take long."

"Well, okay. I've already had my swim. What do you want to know? Like how is it up here in Tahoe? Dullsville. That's how."

"You work at the Gilded Cuckoo in Poway?"

"Yes."

"Were you at the front reception desk Monday morning, Labor Day?"

"Well, sure."

"Do you know Miss Clayton of Rancho Santa Fe?"

"Pamela Clayton? Yes."

"Did she have an appointment there for Monday morning?"

"Yes. It was for ten-thirty. Hair styling. With Mr. K."

"Was she there? Did she keep the appointment?"

"Yes. Right on time."

"You're certain? You saw her there?"

"Sure. Why?"

"Did you see her leave?"

"Well, no. I had an early lunch date."

"But she did leave?"

"She must have—before I got back. Mr. K never takes more than an hour and a half or two, at the most, for a cut, shampoo and set. What she was down for."

"What about a party named Massin with an appointment at the same time—ten-thirty?"

She asked me to spell it and I did. "I never heard of her."

"H. Massin is a man," I said.

"Well, I never heard of him either."

"Has Miss Clayton been there before?"

"Sure. She's a regular customer."

"Just for hair styling?"

"Well, let's say that and other things."

82

Other things, I thought, could have been for overuse of drugs. Clinical therapy. "What about Mrs. Clayton—Monica Clayton?"

"Oh, you mean the old movie star? Monica Moore? I see her once in a while on late TV. Do you know her, too?"

"Yes. Would you consider her a regular at your place?"

"She's been coming here for years."

"Years? More than one?"

"Sure. I've been working there for at least three years. I've seen her lots. And she's been there before I got the job. That place has been there some time, you know. Like years."

"Did she come often?"

"Well, not every week, if that's what you mean. She's in the habit of coming down once in a while and staying over for a few days."

"Was she a patient there? Under treatment?"

"Gee, I don't know. You'd have to ask Mr. Glendon there or some of the doctors. A lot of people come there to take off extra weight, you know. It's a health spa." She giggled. "We starve them and run them ragged until they're back in shape. You'd be surprised what they pay for not eating regular."

"What about alcoholics?"

"We got every kind. Let's face it, that's what keeps spas in business. And the Cuckoo is way out of town. Nobody has to know what you're there for."

"I'd like to come up there, see you and get a statement."

"Okay, sure, if I can help."

"I'll try to get a flight up there tonight."

"Tonight? Crazy! I'll look forward to it. This place has been a real nothing so far. Nobody to talk to."

"Do you always take your vacation at this time?"

"No. Usually earlier. I was overdue, but they kept saying they couldn't spare me, they didn't have the right replacement. Then, all of a sudden, my boss said okay, take off now while it's slow."

"Would that be Mr. Glendon?"

"Yeah. You know him?"

"Yes. When did he decide it was all right for you to start your vacation?"

"Boy, you sure ask a lot of questions. When you come up, we won't have anything left to talk about."

"Sure we will. That's the last question for now."

"Swell. It was Monday, Labor Day. Right after lunch. He said to take off, they didn't need me, have fun, and like that. If he'd told me earlier, I could have been up here for lunch and maybe met somebody before I went for a swim."

"If you haven't made other plans, maybe we could have dinner later tonight."

"What plans? It's like nobody up here knows I'm alive."

"I do," I said. "Hang on. Help is on the way."

"Groovy. I hope you look as good as you sound."

"Better not depend on it."

Her laugh was an infectious giggle. "Try cabin five when you get here. We'll find out."

Lake Tahoe lies between California and Nevada. It is twenty-two miles long and twelve miles wide. Its snow-fed waters are a distinct and beautiful cobalt blue. The Totem Lodge jutted over a part of its northern end and it was too dark when I got there to see the lovely dark blue of the lake. There were several small cabins strung along the lake in the woods, separated from the main lodge building and each other by narrow paths and slender pines.

The cabin light was on, her door ajar. It seemed a nice hospitable gesture. I knocked on the door and called her name. She didn't answer and I had that old, cold feeling and walked in.

Her eyes were wide open and surprised. They had the same dark-blue color as the lake. It was the long knife buried in her back that had surprised her. That and perhaps the swift sudden knowledge that this was all there was going to be of life for Bonnie Burns. Something inside me screamed in anger at this ruthless and wanton waste.

84

She was sprawled on the floor, her red hair damp and darkened with her blood. She was young and would have been beautiful and vibrant alive. I stared at a blond wig set out on her dressing table. I wondered if she had worn it recently. If her killer had mistaken her for another blonde. I took Pam Clayton's photo from my pocket and was disturbed by the near resemblance. Same age. Similar coloring. They could have passed for sisters.

I found her driving license in her purse. Her home address was in Encinitas. That's a beach town not far from Rancho Santa Fe, on the way down to old Del Mar.

Thirteen

The cabins on either side were dark. Others farther away were lit up, alive with laughter and good spirits, blaring rock music into the night. I walked to the dark rim of the lake. A few couples were making out on blankets. A hundred yards out a girl dived off a float. She was quickly joined by another. They swam, splashed and laughed. In the distance, a power boat whined, heading for the other end of the placid lake. It could have been Bonnie's killer. But he could have been anywhere by this time. The girl's body had been as cold as the bone-handled hunting knife between her shoulder blades.

I wondered bleakly if I would find the Clayton kid as still and blood-wetted, and why a killer had taken the trouble to put Willie's head under water and hold it there when a knife or bullet was faster.

I called the local sheriff's office from the main lodge, and they said they'd get a man out. I flushed a cab to the airport. The return plane to L.A. was warming up, but I found out there had been earlier flights out to Reno, San Francisco and Vegas. The killer needn't have waited around for me.

I counted seven passengers. Two women, five men. One of the women had the seat next to her piled high with bags, baskets, containers of all sorts. I put her down as a grand-mother visiting a newly married daughter with a lot of groceries for the family. The second was dark and bulky, her face half covered with a scarf, wearing a thick high-collared coat. She was humming and talking to herself as she stared out the seat window. She had a big ball of wool on the seat and a big pair of knitting needles, scissors and a stack of magazines. Another nut coming to join the relatives in L.A.

I spoke to the men. An elderly reverend gentleman, long retired from the cloth, he said, out of Tahoe City. He told me he was traveling to Los Angeles to meet other members of a protesting committee alarmed about the concentrated build-up in Tahoe of motels, which, to his mind, brought in sin.

The second was a chubby salesman of electric lighting, who had negotiated a big deal on animated neons with one of the large casinos on the lake front. The third was a ranger from the Sequoia National Park quitting the service after twenty years. He couldn't stand the way the young people were using his park's preserves. "No reverence," he said bitterly. "Smoking pot and nailing lanterns to trees. Ruining the bark. Swimming naked in the lake and making love in broad daylight in the meadows. They don't give a damn about ecology, or anything or anybody."

The fourth was a saturnine dental surgeon from San Diego, who said he was dying of cancer at forty-three. He looked more. He said he had come up to see the beautiful blue water of the lake before he went to the big operating room in the sky. He said it used to be a lot bluer, but considering everything what could you expect. A week was all the time he could spare there.

I was the seventh passenger, the only one aboard who looked and felt like a murderer. I stared into the dark at my reflection in the glass until I became sick of it.

After we put down at L.A. International, the women got off first. The woman with the groceries headed for the first phone booth. The humming eccentric with the knitting needles and long shears went for the john. She had left her seat and the floor around it littered with pictures cut out of the magazines.

The retired reverend and the retiring ranger picked up their luggage from the spinning drop in the baggage room. The lighting salesman grabbed his brief case and headed for the bar. The dying dental surgeon and I went directly to the exit and the hack stands. I let him have the first one that came along because he was dying and in more of a hurry.

The ugly dark woman came down the passageway riding the treadmill conveyor belt. She passed me and sprinted across the street at the light change. By the time I realized she had discarded her woolly ball and knitting needles, she had disappeared into the parking lot. A lot of them like that leave more personal items behind them on the benches at the ball parks.

I got back to my apartment and smelled whiskey and trouble. The door had been forced, the living room attacked by a strong, bad-tempered visitor. I knew who it was before I found the note from Lance Kite on my TV set saying he was sorry he had missed me and would try again. The place didn't look any worse than it had after the last earthquake.

I put some of it back together, had a few drinks, and went to bed. There were several mysteries to solve now and I couldn't come close to any satisfying answers. I didn't do any better in my dreams. I ran around all night knocking on the wrong doors, bumping into things, stumbling over dead bodies. Willie kept following me, asking when I was going to take care of his matter.

I dialed Homcide the next morning after coffee and asked for Lieutenant Camino. Nick is a tough, hard-bitten Chicano, an intelligent man who has never fallen for the bravura bit of the big-city cop looking askance at a private eye. He wears his blue-and-gold shield without affectation. We've maintained a good and steady respectful relationship down the years, combined our resources at times, occasionally with good results.

I hoped this might be another of those good times.

He came on gruff but friendly, asking me what kind of trouble I was in now, and I told him.

"Have you killed anybody yet?"

"No. Not yet."

"I heard about Willie Rich," he said softly. "I'm sorry. I heard it was accidental drowning, too. You say you don't have a thing yet?"

"Only a headache."

"Let's have the rest of it."

I told him about the missing Pam and the murdered Bonnie.

"Christ!" he exploded. "Why haven't you called me sooner?"

"It's only been happening since Monday, Nick. What's the matter? What am I missing?"

"A little luck wouldn't hurt."

"If I wait for luck, I'll lose a few more."

"Everything so far is out of my district. What kind of blade was that Tahoe job?"

"Hunting knife. Ivory handle. Not Johnny Cashio's usual style."

"I can check him out for you. What else?"

"Louis Charnock. What do you know about him?"

"He cost me twenty bucks. My wife went to one of his lectures and felt she had to buy some of his books."

"Is he on the level?"

"Who the hell is? Elsie went because she goes for that crap about the formula for personal success, riches and happiness."

"Did it work?"

"Are you kidding? She did it for me, she said. She has the idea policemen are underpaid."

"Maybe it takes time for all those positive thoughts to circulate in the cosmos."

"The board of supervisors and the city council would be a better place. What else is eating you?"

"Charnock's assistant, Wesley Dorn. Plays the pipes at Charnock's stage lecture. Sells the books. Greets the ladies. Do you have anything on him?"

"I run Homicide. Has he killed anybody?"

"I'd like to believe it. He seemed a sharp cookie. Takes care of the money end for Charnock, I imagine."

"So what?" Camino said impatiently. "Charnock needs that kind of help. He does big business. With his kind of income, the IRS will want to be looking over other books than the ones he peddles in the lobby. If you're talking about fraud, that's not my department, either. Talk to the Bunco people or the D.A.'s office."

I mentioned the Bunco bureau report and my visit to Lance Kite. Camino chuckled and asked what I got out of Kite. I told him. "A sore thumb."

He scoffed. "That karate crap is showboating. Come down to my office sometime. I'll show you how to make a real fist."

"I don't need that kind of help. I need direction. I'm getting nowhere fast on this caper. I can't seem to close in."

"Well, what the hell do you expect, hotshot?" he demanded. "You want to break it all in three days? You've been watching too many of those private-eye reruns on TV. You know better than that. You're supposed to be an investigator, for Christ's sake. Get off your tail and do some legwork."

Jim Kilburn was one of the new breed of young whizz ten-percenters, an agent who handled athletes. He had a stable of the country's superstars, footballers, basketballers, big-time winning jocks. Cherubic and innocent-looking, Kilburn belied his bland appearance with a pirate's ruthless regard for scruples. He set stratospheric salary demands for his people and paralyzed club owners and sports operators indiscriminately with the kind of contracts only a loaded operator could deal with. After getting the million-dollar preliminaries over with as front money, Kilburn had additional salt to rub in the wounds by asking for and getting a line of fringe benefits unheard-of before in the areas where the sports jocks had always been highly acclaimed and then treated as peons. Kilburn changed it all with life-style bonuses, tax write-offs, insurance and participant spin-off deals, making his people solvent and the sports magnates only precariously so with one stroke of his pen.

Willie Rich was one of his superstars. Willie got ten percent of his winnings for the owners, and Kilburn got his. I was hoping a bright boy like Kilburn had already calculated his loss and had a line on whoever had dealt a mortal blow to one of his more profitable relationships.

His offices were high over Wilshire, fittingly in a bank building in Beverly Hills, one of the newer high rises. What I could see of his working staff looked to be fugitives from a Vegas line, all lovely in looks and limb. One took me to his room too quickly, leaving me to look with less interest at Kilburn and the pictures of his clients on the walls.

He surprised me as soon as I got to the point, by looking astonished. He had totally accepted Willie's demise as natural, not encouraged by a killer. His baby-blue eyes shifted to the ten-million-dollar gallery of signed gratefuls on his wall. "I hope it's not contagious," he said. Then he gave me the pat stand-by. "Why would anybody want to kill Willie?"

"He represented a lot of money, Kilburn. Maybe somebody was trying to get even with you. Maybe he was incidental."

"That's ridiculous. I've got the people they want and without me they can't do business." He grinned. "Besides, they can't get even. I'm too far ahead."

"You don't have all the people. Only a corner. If you screwed somebody real good lately, there's a chance you left some hostility spilling over after the contract was initialed."

He shook his curly head. "If they wanted revenge, they wouldn't have waited this long. I've had them by the balls for too long. Anyway, it's like you said. I'm not the only lawyer in the sports end of it now. There's lots of company. All the new reps know what I've done and are out for more of the same for their clients, meaning all the traffic can bear."

"Let's take it back to Willie then and see if we can't get a line on who might have wanted him dead."

He wheeled an open file carrier closer and thumbed through it, pulling out a thick manila folder. He threw it down on his large desk and stamped it with his chubby white fist. "Willie operated on his own the first few years. Here's the record since I've had him. Every race, every owner or trainer he got up for, every dime he made. That file goes back fifteen years."

I leafed through the folder. The list of his winnings and earnings were staggering. Ninety hundred-granders. He had made millions for a lot of owners and trainers, and several for himself. The sixty-two hundred career wins he had was fantastic. It reminded me that winning jocks with the highest ratings, like Willie, can be expected to average twenty to twenty-five percent of their mounts in the winner's circle, and that in turn meant he had come down the stretch about twenty-five thousand times.

I looked at Kilburn. "That's an awful lot of times for a man to have his heart in his throat. Even if each time lasted a little over a minute."

Kilburn nodded. "We don't even know how many times he went down to the wire. Willie started riding county-fair tracks when he was fifteen, then Caliente and a lot of other little border towns. I figured he had served his dues and that's why I got every extra dollar for him that I could. He had it coming. But his record of wins made it easy. There wasn't an owner or trainer who wouldn't take him if he was available."

"I'd like a list of every owner and trainer you have down here. Maybe one of them wasn't happy with a ride Willie gave his horse and had to get even."

"I doubt that very much." He smiled. "Everybody knows you can't win them all. Those guys know their percentages."

"Sure they do. But when you have a favorite horse, you tend to forget the figures. With a good horse and Willie up, you expect a win. It's human nature. And human nature says the hell with logic and figures."

He pressed a button on his desk and almost at once a long-legged beauty walked in. Kilburn extracted several sheets from the folder and handed them to her. "Photocopies for Mr. Roper, Sandy, as soon as you possibly can."

"Yes, sir."

"I'll expect them in ten minutes or under."

"Yes, sir."

She went out without looking hurt.

"You didn't even say 'please,' " I said admiringly.

"That'll be the day," Kilburn said. "Getting back to your theory, I suppose I never paid it any mind because no other jock has been knocked off lately. Willie's no different, or wasn't, from the others. More successful than most, no doubt, but Pincay is good, too, and he's still around and healthy, and Shoe, Grant, Pierce and a lot of other good boys. Longden is still living and Arcaro, too. So is Joey Zale. Granting your motive, any or all of them should be dead as well as Willie. They all lost some big ones sometime along the line. They all made some owner and his wife or his trainer unhappy. They all lost a pile of dough for some wise in-the-know hotshot, including a lot of gamblers and syndicate boys. I'll make my point again. They're in the same line as Willie, disappointed an awful lot of people, probably made enemies. They've ridden other jocks into the rails or wide around the turns and picked up some extra hate there, too, if you like. But the fact remains, they're all still here; none of the big ones have been knocked off. I'll have to repeat again, what the hell was so special about Willie Rich?"

"You've made it a good point," I said. "But there are some other factors now." I brought up the disappearance of Clayton's daughter.

Kilburn didn't change expression. "If you'll pardon me, I don't see the connection."

"I heard they've been seeing each other."

"Bullshit," Kilburn said. "She's a nice sort of dopey kid and Willie took her out a couple of times. So did I, for the same reasons, more or less."

"More or less," I repeated. "Which?"

He shrugged. "What the hell's the difference?"

"You're not married. Willie is—or was."

"You think Penny did it, to get even?"

"I don't know who did it. For all I know, maybe you did."

"Maybe I did," he said. "I can't seem to remember the reason."

I slapped the manila folder on his desk. "Over a million reasons right there, Kilburn. Maybe you were screwing Willie on his money. Maybe he found out. Maybe you wanted him not to make any fuss about it and the only way possible was to put his head under water."

Kilburn gave me a nasty look and patted his forehead with a silk hanky. "You're right. That would make a pretty good reason. As a matter of fact, the issue of money has come up between us recently. Not in the way you think, though, and certainly not motivating me toward killing him."

"Sounds interesting," I said. "Fill me in."

"We were discussing a considerable amount of money that I stood to lose. As his agent. He would, of course, have stood to lose considerably more."

"Forget you're a lawyer, Kilburn. Tell me what the hell you're talking about the simplest way you can imagine."

"Okay. Willie told me he didn't want to ride any more of Clayton's horses after the Del Mar season was over. He was willing to buy back the advance and the contract."

"Tyler Clayton's horses? Mrs. Monica Clayton's? Or Miss C.'s?"

"I imagine he meant all of them inclusively. He was talking about Tyler specifically."

"When did he tell you this?"

"About a month ago."

"Before the Del Mar meeting started?"

"Yes. It's considered a big one for the jocks, owners, trainers—everybody."

"Even agents?"

"Even them," he said agreeably. "Willie might have made over a million if he cared to ride what was available. I'd make my ten percent of that, of course."

"Did he offer any reason?"

Kilburn shook his head and said no.

I didn't know any more of Willie's latest financial condition than I knew of Kilburn's. They made an awful lot of money, and still could have blown it and needed more. But Willie apparently wanted out. I thought what the hell, it was his neck and his money. I wished I knew his reason and faced Kilburn again. "Could you figure Willie's reason on your own?" I asked.

Kilburn shook his head. "The only thing I could come up with is boredom. He'd been riding too long. Now he wanted less horses, fewer rides. He didn't talk about retiring. He and Ty Clayton have always got along, to my knowledge. Willie brought in an awful lot of winners for him down through the years. Maybe Clayton didn't need the money, but it certainly brought him what he wanted out of racing."

"What was that?"

"A kind of fame, pride—he likes being a winner. He likes horse racing, too. Breeding—the whole shmeer." He shook his head again. "They never had any trouble before."

"Things may have been different since Clayton married Monica. That could spell the difference right there."

Kilburn smiled indulgently. "If you're thinking Willie and Monica had differences, forget it. You're way off base. They got along fine, too."

"She wanted Willie to ride Sister Sally, her mare, in the Princess Stakes, Labor Day. Willie refused and rode his boss's filly Calamity, as you know. Maybe that didn't make her too happy with Willie."

"Maybe. But not enough for her to go out and kill him."

"That's what she told me," I said.

"It doesn't tie up either with Willie not wanting to wear Clayton's colors any more. Monica wouldn't have been that insistent. She keeps a low profile down there. Doesn't act like any rich power-hung bitch even with the means to do so."

"I'll buy that for the moment," I said. "Maybe Mrs. Clayton has her reasons for playing it quiet and cool down there."

Kilburn sat back straighter in his leather chair. "What the hell does that mean, Roper?"

I shrugged. "She's had a rough life. A lot of tragedy. A lot of unpleasant notoriety."

He smiled. "She also had a pretty big name in Hollywood at one time. She was a front-page international beauty, and she still is, to my mind."

"Mine, too," I said. "And I dig her perfume. A very nice sweet-smelling lady."

He sniffed. "So what's your beef?"

"Nothing large and specific. She used to be tied up in some way with a man called Louis Charnock."

"I've heard of him."

"That was supposed to be a long time ago when her career was breaking up. She's still seeing him."

Kilburn smiled. "So what? Charnock isn't any threat. He sounds like a charlatan, I agree, but I think in his own mind he's doing some good in the world."

"What the hell kind of good can he be doing Monica now? She's got one of the richest men in California. She's in society. What does she need Charnock for now with all she's got?"

Kilburn spread his hands apart. "Well, money isn't everything. Maybe he still gives her spiritual peace."

I was about to suggest that Kilburn discuss this aspect of the Monica Moore–Louis Charnock relationship with Lance Kite, but decided the hell with it. I didn't want to get sidetracked by Monica again. "Getting back to Willie quitting Clayton, isn't it odd that Cap Abbott didn't know about it? I spoke to him the other day."

"Not odd," Kilburn said. "I don't think Willie had told anybody yet but me."

"Not even Clayton?"

He looked concerned for a moment. "Not to my knowledge. You'll have to ask Clayton about that. But assuming that he did, can you see Tyler Clayton drowning him over that?"

I had to admit I couldn't. "Where were *you* Labor Day, Kilburn?"

He smiled. "Not down at old Del Mar. Not killing Willie. I was up in San Francisco negotiating a business deal."

"All day? All night?"

"What hours are you interested in?" he asked.

"Willie was still alive after the eighth race. The guard saw him walk out the jock club door about six. He was killed about ten o'clock. Penny found him in the pool around midnight."

"I know. Allie Riegel phoned me and told me all about it."

"Phoned you where?" I asked. "What time?"

Kilburn swallowed and his blue eyes wavered. "At my home in Bel Air. Two in the morning. I'd taken the early night flight out of San Francisco. PSA. I had a room at the St. Francis."

"My favorite hotel," I said. "Whom did you have business with?"

"The Forty-Niner people. Football business. A new contract for one of my new people. Haywood, the former Dallas Cowboy tight end. Also with the San Francisco Warrior club owners. A new deal for Monaco, former Drake guard."

"Good people," I said. "What early flight did you make?"

"Seven-fifteen."

"Seven-fifteen," I repeated.

"We set down at L.A. International at eight oh five. That left me just enough time to fly down to Escondido and knock Willie off in his pool."

"It's possible," I said. "I know you fly your own plane.

But I guess you didn't because you had a previous engagement."

"Correct."

"You're not going to tell me it was with Pam Clayton?"

"I'm not telling you another goddam thing," he said sharply.

I looked out the windows. "How high up are we?"

"Twenty-three floors. What the hell are you talking about now?"

"I'm still talking about who killed Willie." I stood up. "Either you tell me where the hell you were after eight Monday night, or I'm going to throw you right out of your damn window."

"What the hell are you—some kind of a psycho?"

"Let's find out."

"I'll tell you," he said. "But I wouldn't want it to get around."

"My lips are sealed."

He scribbled a name on a slip of paper and showed it to me. I whistled. "I didn't know you were gay, Kilburn."

His lip curled. "I'm not. I needed Haywood's signature on the new contract. That's the club where I met him."

I remembered the player. Big, rough, exceptionally good with his hands. "You mean Haywood—?"

"I had to tell you in self-defense," Kilburn snapped. "If word of this gets around, I'll sue you for defamation of character."

"Are you telling me the other fruits at this Golden Grotto don't who who he is?"

He threw up his hands. "Well—maybe. I trust that answers your question. Maybe you have another?"

"A girl named Bonnie Burns. Worked at the Gilded Cuckoo in Poway. Would you happen to know if she knew Willie?"

"I never heard of her. I know Willie used the spa at times to sweat off a few pounds if he got over one hundred twelve. What's the connection?"

"I don't know if there is one. I found her murdered last night up at Lake Tahoe. Knife in her back."

He sat up stiffly, shaken. "Christ! What for?"

"I don't know yet. If your girl has finished those photocopies, I'll get out of here."

He picked up his phone and inquired. "All set. You can pick them up at the reception desk on your way out." He hesitated. "I wish I could be of more help to you about Willie."

"You've helped," I said. "You've convinced me you didn't kill Willie. That's one less to worry about."

Fourteen

There were a lot of owners and trainers on Kilburn's list with longer and better track records than Tyler Clayton, better horses and larger stables. But he was the only one who had reported a missing daughter on the same day Willie Rich was drowned.

I eased into his curved driveway later in the day. There wasn't any sign of a green fastback Mustang, and I got out and started for the front door. A sudden fusillade of shots came from behind the big white house and I veered off, ducking low, skirted a garden wishing well and ran around a thick hedge toward the sounds of battle.

I skidded around the corner, and put up my snub-nosed .38, feeling had. All that was getting killed was a regulation close-combat silhouette target. The law-and-order people usually work out on this one, but Tyler Clayton had enough money to invent his own games and play at them.

He stood facing a small outdoor shooting range, firing at a full-front Prell dummy. He was chopping holes in at thirty yards and hitting the high numbers over the vital spots. Clayton saw me out of the corner of his eye and snapped off two fast ones that gave him a six-pointer for the groin and an eight for the stomach. He already had a few nines over the heart and a good four above the eyes.

I could tell a rugged individualist like Tyler Clayton had no intention of calling in the FBI to find his daughter if he could do the job himself. There were boxes and clips of ammunition stacked on a range table, an automatic twelve-gauge shotgun, and several other expensive-looking handguns, sight scopes and holsters. Several frame targets with the bull's-eye centers well perforated with accurate fire had been discarded and leaned against the side. It looked like graduation day at the FBI school.

Clayton grinned widely, spun the gun like Billy the Kid, and faked a quick draw. "Care to try your luck?"

"No, thanks," I said. "I think I just had it."

"Go on," he insisted. "Try it."

He extended the gun to me butt first. It was a handsome Colt Python .357 Magnum, a gun developed for police use. Its load would penetrate both armor and glass. It also had enough penetration to shoot through a car from the rear, with power left to kill the driver.

I shook my head. "Sorry. I can't get mad at a target."

"You can't afford to miss either, son, when you have to shoot. Practice takes care of it. I've a good collection of shooting rifles inside if that would suit your pleasure better."

"Not today. I was just passing through. I wondered if you had heard anything from your daughter."

He looked at me, cheeks flushed. "Not a goldurn word."

"No messages? No phone calls? Nothing?"

"You got it right the last time, son. Nothing."

He whirled toward the target again and snapped off a quick shot from the hip. It put a hole an inch to the right of the black center x. That gave Clayton a ten and whoever might have been facing him a permanent pass to the big shooting gallery up in the sky. He grinned, winked at me, reloaded, then slipped the shooter into a shoulder-rig holster and jerked it into place.

"Do you carry that gun on you usually?" I asked.

"Sometimes."

"That happens to be a pretty effective and deadly

weapon. It's one of the few handguns around that can surely kill a man."

He nodded. "I know, son."

"You can't be certain yet your daughter has been kidnapped. You might kill somebody by mistake."

"When I kill somebody, son, it's no mistake." He smiled, jutting his big chin toward the target. "I've had plenty of practice shooting. Grew up with a gun in my hand, an old shotgun, or sometimes a rifle of my daddy's."

"Where was this, Texas? I guess they do start them shooting when they're young down there."

"Hell, no. Not Texas. Saskatchewan."

"Canada?"

"Yes, sir. Grew up there. Did plenty of hunting when we were kids—me and my brothers. A lot of game up there, son."

"Rabbits?"

"Some. Also fox, moose and bear. Got me my first grizzly when I was fourteen." He stood there huge, proud, remembering a big kill.

A kid that age had to be mighty reckless to tackle a grizzly. He might have been big then. Even so, he had to be a little crazy.

Clayton extended his hands out flat, palms down. "How about that? I always had a good eye and a steady hand."

I was glad he didn't want to make it a contest.

He smirked confidently. "Yes, sir. Been a hunter all my life. Hunted big game. Hunted gold. Hunted oil. Ever do any of those, son?"

I said no, I hadn't.

"Then you've missed a lot of fun."

"My business is hunting people." It sounded a tired cliché.

His glance was sly. "I reckon you're talking about killing."

"If I have to."

He grinned. "How many men have you killed, son?"

"I forget," I told him.

About to answer, his eyes shifted over my shoulder. His expression and voice softened. "Hi, sweetheart. You just come home?"

Monica Clayton was walking toward us from the terrace. "A little while ago," she answered huskily. She walked with a sinuous grace, erect, gently swaying. Her figure would still drive a lot of younger women to cover. "I heard shooting. Was that you, Tyler?" She stopped a few steps away and met my eyes. "Hello, Mr. Roper. It's good to see you again. I hope you've some good news for us about Pam."

I looked at her carefully. She was dressed casually but very expensively in fine country threads. Well-groomed. She didn't look at all worried. "Are you serious?" I asked.

She flushed. "What do you mean?"

"All I got was the little four-by-five picture off the desk. Apart from that, neither of you gave me anything to help find her. No description. No background. I assume she's gone to school, maybe had some girl or boy friends. At twenty-two, if nothing's wrong with her, she's bound to have some habits, hangouts, some hints as to her normal procedure. You've got to be kidding."

She flinched and stepped back. Clayton growled. "Now, lookee here—" He had lapsed easily into his backwoods English.

"Money talks, mister," I added. "And with your kind of dough, you can do damn near anything. If you took your daughter's disappearance seriously, you'd have brought the FBI in, the local fuzz, the whole damn combined forces of the law-and-order reps in the country.

"No. You don't want your kid found. Not yet, anyway. You have your reasons, maybe. If so, that's your business. But you're playing a dangerous game. It could kick off and explode right in your face."

Clayton purpled. "I told you I wanted her found, didn't I? Jest because you been dragging your ass don't mean you can turn it on me. What's holding you up—money?" He wheeled on the woman behind him. "Bring me my checkbook, Monica. Maybe that's what he needs to convince him I mean business."

"Don't bother," I said angrily. "I found a murdered girl up at Lake Tahoe last night. She wasn't your daughter, but she could have been. Your money now is no guarantee your kid will be found alive."

I had their attention now. Monica Clayton showed me how she could part her lips and breathe deeply. The surly old oil baron clenched his fists and looked longingly at the Colt in his holster.

"This girl lived around here. She worked at your favorite spa—the Gilded Cuckoo. Maybe you know her, Mrs. Clayton—the receptionist—Bonnie Burns?"

Her shoulders sagged on cue. "Bonnie—dead?" Her lips quivered, her voice shook in a lower register. "Was she drowned—too?"

"No. This job wasn't like Willie's. She had a knife in her back."

Clayton put his arm around her waist. His slate eyes narrowed angrily. "What the hell's this got to do with my kid? Maybe this Bonnie worked at the spa. I don't know her. What the heck you driving at now, mister?"

"She could have been murdered by mistake," I said. "She's about the same age as your daughter. Looks a lot like her, too, judging from the picture I have. The thing that puzzled me was that although she was a natural redhead, Bonnie Burns had a blond wig.

"She left the Gilded Cuckoo on her vacation Monday afternoon. About the same time your daughter was supposed to be there. I don't know why she wore the blond wig. Maybe the killer didn't know either. Maybe he thought she was your daughter when he put the knife into her back."

Monica Clayton tossed her strawberry-blond hair out of its set and stamped her heel. "You're wrong. Pam never did get to the spa for her hair appointment. I checked there.

They told me she hadn't been there Monday. She didn't even have an appointment. She lied to me."

"Why would she lie about a hair appointment?" I asked.

"I don't know."

"There's another possibility," I said. "Bonnie Burns was at her reception desk at the Gilded Cuckoo spa Monday morning. If Pam came in and did keep an appointment, Bonnie saw her. If somebody there wanted that kept a secret, they took care of it the best way there is. Bonnie can't tell anybody now whether your daughter was there or not."

Clayton was dancing a jig in his high-heeled western boots. "If what you're telling me is the truth, mister, I'll go down there and tear that place apart." Suddenly he brought his big fist down on the table, bouncing the expensive firearms apart. "But hold on now—hold on—there's something wrong with what you're saying, mister."

I waited for him to figure it out. It didn't take too long.

"There's an easy way of checking these things, ain't there? They keep appointment books, don't they, for this kind of thing?"

I nodded. Mrs. Clayton kept me company.

"Well, then," he said, smiling shrewdly, "the simplest thing is to jest check their books. That'll tell us all we want to know—if Pam was there or not, or even had that danged appointment in the first place."

"I did that already," I said. "Tuesday morning. I had Mr. Glendon who's in charge there show me the book."

"Well?" Clayton demanded.

"She wasn't down. She had no appointment."

Clayton stared at me, all the fire gone. "So she never had no reason to go there in the first place. So what the hell are we talking about?"

"There's another possibility," I said. "If somebody wanted your daughter kept out of the way, for any reason, they'd also be smart enough to fix up the appointment book. That wouldn't be difficult. It was a loose-leaf affair."

"I don't understand," Monica Clayton said huskily. "Why would anybody want Tyler's daughter kept out of the way, as you suggested?"

I gave her my million-dollar shrug. "Maybe she knows something."

Clayton snorted angrily. "Bullfeathers! What the hell would she know?"

"Maybe I'll still be able to find her," I said. "Then, if she's still alive, maybe she'll tell me."

When I left, Clayton had his arm around his wife's waist. She leaned against him and her beautiful head was jammed against his chest. I hoped she didn't make his pistol go off by accident and give me another killing to solve.

Fifteen

I headed west for the Pacific Coast Highway, wondering when I'd get a break, a lead to something tangible. At the edge of the village, I found it. A new shopping center sprawled over a large city block. A slim dark-haired girl I recognized was wheeling a shopping cart along the parking lot. I drove in. She was putting her grocery bags into a red Toyota when I parked alongside and got out. "Hello. Aren't you the Claytons' maid?"

She flashed me a friendly smile. "Maid, *ja*. Cook, too, and now I am shopping for dinner. You are the policeman who came the other day, no?"

"Detective. I'd like to ask you some questions, Miss—"

"Pauli. Pauli Lundgren. What questions?"

"About your mistress—Pam—Miss Clayton."

"You have no word about her yet?"

"No. Perhaps you can help. Tell me things about her."

"What can I tell you? I am working there just a little past one year. Since the other Mrs. Clayton died."

"Do you know what she died of?"

She put a hand over her heart. I couldn't see her heart, but her breast was beautiful. "She was a very sick woman," Pauli said in her singsong way.

"You were there when she died?"

"Yes. The last month. My father in Sweden was a doctor, so I know a little about being a nurse, too. I helped out. Miss Pammy liked me and I her, so I stayed on."

"Did she ever disappear like this before?"

"Disappear, no. She was away. She was going to college."

"Where?"

"The UC San Diego. She is just graduated."

"I thought all Swedish maids said 'yoost.' "

"They are the ones from Denmark."

"How did Pam get along with her new mother?"

"Mrs. Monica?" She looked down at her ankles. They looked fine. Her legs were even better. "It is not right I should talk about people I work for."

"I'm trying to get an idea how things were at the house. If they were bad enough to make the girl want to run away."

"Oh, yes, I see that. It is what a detective should ask."

"Okay, I'm asking. Was the girl unhappy since her father remarried?"

"Not right away. But, yes—in a few months. They did not talk to each other much. No fighting. Only to pass time politely. Like strangers, I think."

"Did Pam have many friends? Go out a lot?"

"Friends, not too many. Some, yes. Lately she is going out more. Almost every night since graduation."

"Do you have any idea where she goes?"

"She is a very rich girl, no? She goes to a lot of parties."

"Did you know Willie Rich?"

"The jockey for Mr. Clayton? No. That is too bad for him to die that way."

"Are you telling me the truth, Pauli? Willie Rich must have come to the Clayton house sometime."

She shook her head. "Not since Pauli is working there."

I wondered about that. "Unless I've been getting the wrong information, I thought Willie Rich had been seeing Miss Clayton."

She didn't bat her large gray eyes. "Outside, maybe. But this is what you are saying. I do not know."

"Would you know if he ever called her on the phone?"

"Oh, yes. They talk many times that way. But jockeys are little men, no? Small like boys?"

"Yes. Five feet or so. An inch or two either way."

She smiled. "Perhaps that is why he did not come to the house. Mr. Clayton is a very large man. Bigger than you, even."

"That shouldn't have made any difference," I said. "Willie spent his entire life with people bigger than he was. He was a champion. One of the top men in his field. Those horses he rode were a lot bigger than he was, too, and he wasn't afraid of them."

She bit her lip. I would have liked to do it for her. "Ach! I am sorry to be so stupid. Willie was a friend of yours?"

I nodded. "I understand what you were trying to say. Tyler Clayton isn't just a big man. He throws his weight around."

"Very big. Very loud. Always in the temper."

"Okay. We know Clayton. Getting back to cases—has anything happened at the Clayton house recently that struck you as strange?"

"Strange?"

"Out of the ordinary. Something different. Something that could account for Miss Clayton's disappearance."

"Yes, there was something strange. Two things." She turned her wrist up to glance at her watch. "I do not have much time."

"Two things, you said. That shouldn't take long."

"One thing was letters. They made Mr. Clayton very angry."

"Letters? When was this?"

"It started soon after they were married. After Mrs. Monica came to the house."

"The letters were addressed to Mr. Clayton?"

"Yes. They come regularly, one a month."

"Would you know what was in them?"

"How would I know that? Does he read his letters to his maid?"

"What else can you tell me about them? Was there a return address you might remember?"

"No return address, no. But they are mailed from Mexico."

"You said Mr. Clayton became angry. Did he say anything you would recall?"

"Something one time. About how he was not going to let somebody twist him around a finger."

I wondered if Louis Charnock and Monica Moore were revamping an old act. "Did he ever discuss the letters with Mrs. Clayton?"

"I have not heard. But lately there have been no more."

"Do you think they concerned young Miss Clayton?"

"He said nothing to her that I know." She glanced at her timepiece again.

"That's the one thing? Okay, now the other."

"I will tell you if it helps, so nothing bad will happen to young miss. First there were phone calls."

"For her?"

"At first, no. For the master. But he becomes very angry, he shouts a lot and hangs up."

"You don't know who called? The party didn't give his name?"

"No. But I remembered his voice. Later he would call again. This time he would ask for Miss Clayton."

"Did she speak to the caller?"

"Only one time, but just for a moment. Her father heard. He came into her room very red in the face and shouting. He almost breaks the telephone, he puts it down so hard. Then he is telling her she is not to take any more calls from this person."

It could mean something. It could mean nothing. "That's it?"

"There is some more. A few weeks ago—two weeks—a man came to the house. A stranger, *ja*. He is looking around very carefully. He asks is Miss Clayton home. Pamela, he says, not Pam. I say the truth, she is not. He says when will she be home and I cannot say for sure. Then he asks when Mr. and Mrs. Clayton will be home. I do not know that for certain, either. I know they have gone to look at some horses, and I tell him this."

"Did he give you his name?"

"He is about to. But then he changes his mind and he writes down something very fast on a piece of paper from a notebook. He gives it to me and says, please it is for Miss Clayton. Miss Pamela."

"Did you see what he wrote?"

"Numbers. A telephone number. He writes something under it and folds it when he gives it to me."

"He didn't give you any idea who he was?"

"No. Only for Miss Pamela to get the message."

"Did she get it?"

"I left it on the dresser in her room. But I think she did not get it."

"Old man Clayton got there first?"

"I think it was Mrs. Monica. I am not sure, but she was upstairs first. When I asked Miss Pam later if she got the note, she looked at me. 'What note?' she asked. Then she became very pale. Very quiet."

"She didn't ask either her father or stepmother about it?"

"I did not hear anything."

"Can you tell me what this stranger looked like?"

"A big man. Like you, but—" She put her hands to her trim stomach, flattening it even more. "Very thin here."

I was getting the message from all concerned. The flab would have to go. "What kind of car did he drive?"

"No car. He came by taxi. It was waiting for him down at the end of the drive."

I looked at her. She licked her lips and glanced anxiously again at her watch. "That's it? The two things?"

"Yes. Now I must hurry back to prepare dinner."

"One more question, Pauli. Labor Day—Monday. Where were Mr. and Mrs. Clayton that evening?"

"At home. We had a very big party. He wins a very important horse race, no?"

"Yes. Willie Rich won it. Clayton just owned the horse. Was Miss Clayton at the party?"

"No, sir." She smiled again and turned to open her car door. "I yoost remembered something," she said and colored violently.

" 'Yoost' isn't so bad if you remember something important."

Her head bobbed excitedly. "I know what the man said when he was leaving. He said it once more to the cabdriver. He said he was at the Rover House, if miss wanted him. To the cabby, he said, 'Okay, back to the Rover.' "

I took her arm and pulled her close to me. "I'll have to ask another favor of you, Pauli. Don't tell anybody what you just told me."

"Hokay. Now you will find Miss Pam?"

I shook my head. "Now I'm going to kiss you for helping a tired old operative."

She didn't protest, and after I put her back in her car, she stared at me. "Do you always look angry when you kiss a girl?"

I shook the old tired head. It was buzzing with notions. The folklore about Swedish girls. "Only when I don't have time to do a better job."

"It is the same with me when I am cooking," she said gravely.

The Rover House was on the outskirts of old Del Mar. I asked the dude behind the registration desk if anybody had blown in from Mexico within the past few weeks.

"We have a Mr. Hunter," he said.

"Hunter?"

"Mr. Thomas Hunter. From Acapulco."

"Is he in?"

He rubbed his jaw. "Sorry. No."

I asked if the party had checked out and again he shook his head. I asked him then when he had last seen the gentleman from Mexico.

"He left early Labor Day morning," he said.

Sixteen

I was ahead of the railbirds and form-sheet jugglers. Del Mar was yawning, getting up and ready for another day. The hay smelled good as I walked past the stalls. The sleekly groomed horses whinnied and pawed the ground nervously. I couldn't see what they had to be nervous about. They weren't running behind two unsolved murders and a missing person.

Joey Zale glanced up and smiled crookedly when he saw me in the stall opening. He was taping up a nag's foreleg. "This one's a real lady," he told me. "Never tries to kick me."

"Ask her if she has a friend. Can we talk, Joey?"

He patted the young mare's foreleg gently and whispered something soft. The horse nodded and pawed the ground as if testing the new bandage. It whinnied, telling Zale it worked fine. Zale got to his feet, stepped outside, and lit a cigarette. "How's it going? You getting anywhere?"

"If I am, I don't know it. Did Pam Clayton spend much time down here?"

"Yeah. Quite a bit. We got that filly of hers, you know. Mary Jane. Good two-year-old."

"How did she act? Throw her weight around?"

"No. The kid never made waves. You'd never know she

was worth a zillion on the hoof. Nobody knew she was alive."

"They still don't."

"She'll turn up. Hell, it's only been three days."

"I found one last night that only took twelve hours."

He scowled. "A stiff?"

"Kid from around here. Shiv in her back. She could have made some man happy."

"Maybe she did," he growled. "But I can't figure anybody knocking off the Clayton kid. I mean, what for? What's the percentage?"

"Like you said, it could be for kicks. Let's have it, Joey. You've been holding out."

"You're punchy," he said. "What the hell would I know?"

"I understand a stranger's blown into town. He's been trying to contact Clayton's kid. I figure a smart operator would track her down here once he found out horses are her hobby."

He looked up, frowning. "Where'd you get that?"

"There's more, Joey. This dude came straight from Mexico. He checked in at the Rover House. He's been trying to see Pam. He's also been missing since Labor Day morning."

Zale smacked a gnarled fist into his open hand.

"Any time you're ready, Joey."

"Willie set it up," he said. "I don't think the dude is exactly a stranger. I think Willie knew him from away back."

"Willie set what up?"

"The guy came down here a couple of weeks ago. I'm not sure if he met Clayton's kid here or not. Maybe, but I don't know about that. All I know about is Labor Day, and I know about that because Willie told me."

"I still don't know what the hell you're talking about, Zale."

"The Clayton kid had a morning appointment at the Gilded Cuckoo spa out in Poway. Willie must have set it up for the dude to meet her here and he forgot about her beauty-parlor bit. So he dropped over here early that morning to give me the message to forward to the guy. That she wasn't stiffing him on purpose, but that she had this other operation going, see?"

"A man named Hunter?"

"Yeah. I guess. It seems old man Clayton wasn't keen about them getting together. So, like I said, Willie set it up.

"Hunter shows up here a little after ten. He looked a little put out when the kid wasn't here. So I told him what Willie said. He took off right away."

"For the Gilded Cuckoo? To meet her there?"

Zale shrugged. "He didn't say. He just split."

"The kid's been missing since. Hunter, too. Do you think they went off together?"

"Beats the hell out of me. He was old enough to be her old man. He wasn't no kid. Maybe he was an uncle or something. He kind of acted like one."

"The other Mrs. Clayton's brother?"

"I dunno. If you ask me, he looked more like Clayton."

"Can you describe him?"

"Tall man. Thin. Big hands. In his fifties. Tough-looking. Could have been a fighter. Knife scar on his cheek. His nose is broke. Kind of quiet, though. Don't talk much."

"Okay, Joey. You're telling me Willie set it up. He's dead now and won't talk. What I have to know is, did Clayton's kid want to meet him? Did she ever meet him?"

The little man shook his head. "I can't give you that, pal. I don't know. But I figure Willie was straight. If he said it was okay, then it was okay."

"It's good to hear you speaking well of Willie. I hear he took away a pretty good record you once rang up."

Zale spat. "Records, shit, man. Maybe what you didn't hear was when I was all busted up, Willie paid the hospital bills. Willie got me the job here with Abbott. Maybe it don't look like much of a job, but horses always been my life. And I'm still around them. Anyway, I still got one mark up. Willie would have taken it for sure. But he didn't. So I still got that, whatever good it does me."

"It does you a lot of good, Joey," I said, "if you didn't knock off Willie."

"Yeah," he said. "Which reminds me. You were supposed to be working on that one. But you're spending all your time looking for Clayton's kid. Maybe you're being faked out on that play."

"Maybe. Tell me, did Miss Clayton ever come here with a girl about her age, called Bonnie Burns? A redhead."

"Not that I can remember. Why?"

"She's the one somebody knifed up in Tahoe last night."

"You said before she comes from around here. Where?"

"Encinitas. She worked at the Gilded Cuckoo."

Zale whistled and fanned his fingers. "What the hell are you doin' here for, askin' a lot of dumb questions?"

I didn't tell him because I was a pretty dumb detective.

I drove past Poway and headed for La Costa, a very swank golf resort. A few twosomes were tooling around the course in orange golf carts. A lot of the greens had no action at all. A silver-haired elderly gent was off to one side in a shagging area watching a fat duffer shank shot after shot. He kept on nudging the balls over with his toe and the duffer kept putting them off to the range on the right.

I lit a cigarette and waited. The old pro saw me, excused himself, and walked over.

"Mr. Kenevan?"

He admitted it. He looked very fit and bronzed for a man in his late sixties.

I told him my name and profession. "Willie Rich was an old friend. I'm trying to find out why he's dead. I understand he spent a lot of time with you."

Kenevan had a five-iron in his big hands. He thudded the blade into the ground with steel wrists. "I never thought for a minute he drowned himself, either accidentally or on purpose," he said in a high rasping voice. "Willie got too much of a bang out of living to put an end to it himself. Hell, he was only a kid. Just past forty."

"I understand he was spending less time riding the ponies and more time with you lately. Any idea why?"

The old gent grinned. "He knew a good teacher when he found one, I reckon."

"Okay, so you're good. What made Willie decide to take up the game? It probably cost him a couple of grand a week not to be riding home winners."

Kenevan's light-blue eyes crinkled. "Well, you might say he had enough of riding home winners. Golf was another game to him. Something new that he found out he could be pretty good at."

"Was he good?"

"He could have been playing to scratch in another year or so. You know, even though Willie was a little man, he had big hands. Like me. He could hit the ball a long way."

"That's a pretty good reason. Does Pam Clayton belong to this club, by any chance?"

Kenevan nodded. "Indeed she does. Pretty fair golfer, too. One of my best pupils."

It sounded like another good reason.

"I guess Miss Clayton brought Willie to you?"

Kenevan grinned again. "Then you'd be guessing wrong, mister. It was her mother."

"Monica Clayton?"

He shook his head. "The first Mrs. Clayton. Audrey."

"How long ago was that?"

"Five years, or thereabouts."

"She played herself?"

"Damn fine golfer. Got her girl to play when she was a junior."

"I'd heard she was a sickly woman."

He snorted. "Audrey? Don't you believe it. Thin, maybe. But wiry. Strong as a horse."

"How old was she when she died?"

He frowned. "Not very old, and that's a fact. Mid-forties, I'd guess."

"Kind of young for somebody strong as a horse to die. Don't you agree?"

The iron head thudded into the ground again. "You're damn right. I was sure surprised. Had no idea she had a bad heart."

"She seemed in reasonably good health the times you saw her?"

"Perfect. She played at least three times a week, sometimes more. Never rode a cart. Always walked the eighteen holes." He jerked his head contemptuously toward the brace of golfers careening down the adjacent fairway in their go-cart. "Not like those hothouse flowers."

"Would you know Audrey Clayton's maiden name?"

"I'm not certain. It might have been Parker."

I asked him if she had a brother. Kenevan didn't know.

"How about Mr. Clayton? Did he play?"

Kenevan laughed. "Oh, he tried it a couple of times. But he couldn't hack this game. A big man with a lot of power, but he never had the patience for it. He threw his clubs in the lake over by the fourteenth after putting three balls in a row in there. He walked off and never came back."

"But he let his wife and daughter continue playing?"

Kenevan looked surprised. "Of course. All he did was pay for it. What's money to him?"

"Did Tyler Clayton take any lessons from you?"

Again that boyish grin. "No, sir. He figured as how the game was so simple, just a little white ball sitting there, anybody could hit it."

"Let's get back to Willie again. The first Mrs. Clayton got him started at the game. He took lessons from you here. He played here, too. Did he join your golf club?"

"Certainly. Willie belonged to a lot of clubs. Maybe you're forgetting, he had plenty of money, too."

"I'm getting at something else. Did he play here with Pam Clayton?"

"Once in a while, yes. She'd been playing a lot longer, but as I said, Willie hit a long ball. He had a nice touch around the greens, too, and was a good putter. This year he was giving her two strokes a side."

"When did they play?"

"Sunday, sometimes. The track's closed and school is out. Sometimes, if he didn't have a race, they'd play after school."

"You probably knew Willie was married, Mr. Kenevan. How do you think all that golfing went over with Willie's wife, Penny?"

He shrugged. "If you ask me, she didn't care a hoot. For that matter, Willie never seemed to care what she was up to, as I understand it."

"I may be pressing you, but do you think Willie was in love with Clayton's kid?"

The blue eyes narrowed. "I wouldn't say that. It looked a little more the other way around. Pam idolized Willie. She's crazy about horses, you know, and she always regarded Willie as the world's eighth wonder. He liked her, sure. But I'd say it was for laughs."

"How about Tyler Clayton? Did he laugh much over it?"

"Well, now," the old pro said carefully, "I'm not sure that Mr. Clayton knew much about it. He's never around here and we don't go around advertising what twosomes are out on the golf course."

"But it is possible that he found out?"

"Sure. Anything's possible." The eyes leveled on mine and seemed suddenly a lot colder. "Why? D'ya think Clayton dropped Willie?"

"No. I was just considering the possibility."

"You're the detective," he said. "I don't think Clayton would have knocked Willie off for paying too much attention to his daughter. I don't think he would have done anything. Bringing home a new wife created enough of a rift between them."

I supposed that it might. I still wasn't too sure about

whether Tyler Clayton gave a thought toward anything other than his own immediate concern. His daughter was old enough now to be living her own life. Latching on to Monica Moore was an indication that he still intended living his. The tangled threads of her old life, it seemed to me, would in any event certainly pose more of a threat to him than Willie Rich, or any suitor his daughter might have come up with. I knew if I were Clayton and gunning for anybody, my man would be Louis Charnock.

Kenevan was looking at the portly duffer he had left to his own resources. The man was swinging violently, digging up big clods of dirt and grass with each lunge, squirting the ball off in all directions. "Isn't that something?" Kenevan said softly. "They kill Willie and let something like that around taking up time and space." He flipped his iron up and down a few times. "He's a pretty important new member, and if I don't get back there soon, he'll be chewing me out. Have we finished?"

"We have," I said, "unless you can come up with somebody who might have wanted Willie dead."

He squeezed his big hands spasmodically. "Mister, if I knew that, and how to get to him, you wouldn't have a case to be working on."

I didn't want to spoil his day by telling him Clayton's kid was missing. I thanked him and we shook hands, and I let him go back to his duffer.

Seventeen

Business hadn't slowed noticeably at the Gilded Cuckoo, judging from the number of cars lining the parking lot. I didn't see any green fastback Mustangs. I was becoming irritated with the missing girl, with the Claytons' unorthodox approach toward handling it, with myself for becoming involved with a case that didn't make any sense. I was drawn back again because of what Joey Zale had told me. Willie must have had a reason for what he had arranged, assuming Zale was telling the truth. The murder of Bonnie Burns was linked with the farrago somehow, I thought. A cover-up killing I had to unravel.

I took my light traveling bag out of my car and walked through the heavy gilded doors again. The leggy gray-eyed Miss Hill I had seen at the reception desk before was gone. In her place was another of the same mold, young, cute and friendly.

I looked surprised. "Hello. Where's Bonnie?"

Her surprise seemed a lot more genuine. "Bonnie?"

"Bonnie Burns. She used to work here."

"Oh. I don't know her. I'm new here."

"How about Miss Hill? Is she around?"

"Yes. But I think she went back to therapy. Can I help you?"

122

I looked her over carefully. There was no subterfuge in those young guileless eyes. "When did you start being a receptionist here?"

She smiled. "This is my very first day. Do you have an appointment?"

"Only a standing one," I said. She looked puzzled. I held my bag higher. "I spoke to Mr. Glendon the other day. I said I might be back for some of the courses."

"Oh, you mean live-in?" She reached for a leather-bound book. "I don't know if we have a vacancy. Do you know for how long?"

I shook my head. "It all depends. I suppose Mr. Glendon would know more about that."

She opened the book and showed me she wasn't any helper in a secret white-slave ring by running her manicured finger down long columns of names. Opposite them were designated house-group areas and numbers. I wanted very much to look over the list but figured I'd get to that later.

She picked up her phone, asked me my name, and pressed a button. "Mr. Roper is here, Mr. Glendon. He's here to start those courses. Yes, a live-in. I told him I didn't know—" She nodded, listened and hung up. "He'll be right out, sir."

She directed me toward the smaller reception room and I was hardly inside before Glendon arrived. He cocked his head, looking pleased and quite surprised. "Ah, Mr. Roper. Do I understand correctly that you are serious this time?"

"I was serious the other time, too," I said. "But I had to make sure I could take enough time off from my outfit."

"I understand." His eyes looked blandly inquisitive. "I don't believe you told me what business you were in."

"Insurance," I said. "We sell insurance." I patted my midriff. "At my last examination, the company doctor told me I was ten pounds overweight. That's when I decided I had to do something about it."

He nodded briskly. "Good. You look reasonably fit. I don't believe you'll have much of a problem. A week or two.

Hard exercise, limited diet, our mineral water. Pleasant surroundings. No liquor. No smoking. Is that agreeable to you?"

I smiled. "You're the doctor. Whatever it takes."

"Hmm." He was glancing at a sheet of paper. "We don't have the best possible accommodation available right now. But we do have a room that should be comfortable enough." He looked at my traveling bag. "Are you ready to check in now?"

I nodded and took out my wallet. "A down payment now, I suppose?"

He surprised me by shaking his head, fending off the wallet with his hand as if it bothered him to take money. "That's not necessary now. We can bill you later."

He turned as if the matter were settled and opened the inside door. Over his shoulder, he asked, "By the way, that girl you asked about last time—Miss Clayton—I suppose she's returned home by now?"

"I imagine so," I said. "I've been so busy since, I haven't had time to check."

"Well, there you are," he said airily. "It never pays to get excited over these things. I was certain it was all a misunderstanding."

"I suppose. But the Claytons seemed worried. It seemed the least I could do was check with you about it."

"Of course." He led me down a narrow carpeted hallway and out a side door. He entered another building. A husky white-suited attendant rose from behind a small desk. Glendon flipped a thumb over his shoulder. "Ernie, this is Mr. Roper. He'll be staying with us for several days. I've assigned him room number six for the time being."

Ernie shook hands and looked me over. "Weight problem? A little too much boozing?"

Glendon tittered. "Ernie has seen them all, Mr. Roper. You can't hide any secrets from him."

I sighed and looked glum. "I suppose I can live without it. For a few days, anyway. Are we starting now?"

Glendon reached for my bag. "Indeed we are. We'll just

check this over to make sure you haven't brought anything with you. They usually do, you know."

He plucked out the spare fifth I usually carried. "What have we here?" he asked archly. "I thought you were serious about this, Mr. Roper."

I grinned weakly. "I am. But in my case, as I tried to tell you, drinking is a serious problem."

He tossed the bottle to the blond attendant. "It needn't be. Take care of that for Mr. Roper, Ernie. When he leaves, he may have it back if he wishes."

Ernie laughed and set it on the desk. "Maybe he won't want it. Maybe he'll kick the habit this time."

"Let's hope so," Glendon said. He faced me, forefinger up. "It won't be easy. You'll have to try to cooperate. Once you get through the first day, it won't be nearly as difficult."

I shrugged. "I'm here. Might as well give it a whirl."

"Good boy," Glendon said, pleased. "Come on, then. We'll get you settled."

I took a last look at my fifth of Scotch on Ernie's desk. He grinned hugely. Glendon was walking quickly down the hall, swinging my bag, and I followed him again. He stopped abruptly and opened a door. It was a pleasant room even with the bars outside the windows. Apparently they knew at the Gilded Cuckoo how desperate dipsos could get for a drink.

"It's still early enough for you to get started," Glendon said. He tossed my bag on the bed. "I'll leave you alone long enough for you to get into your pajamas. Then we'll head over to the gym and find you some sweat pants for your workouts."

I managed to look surprised. "Pajamas? At this time?"

Glendon smiled. "Your clothing will be returned to you. You understand, of course, that we must remove all incentives for you to leave if the going gets tough."

I shrugged, and started to discard my jacket. Glendon indicated the large closet. "You can put everything in there." He showed me the lock on the door. "Then we'll lock it up and if you're a good boy, we'll let you have it again when you're ready to leave."

I smiled forlornly to show him I was going to be a good sport about it. "You guys think of everything."

"We have to, Mr. Roper. We have to. We're very serious here about your health. Naturally, we've had to deal with experts in deception down through the years. So we take every possible precaution. The discipline may seem harsh, but I'm sure you'll agree it's for your own best interests."

With that, he walked out and I continued undressing. I was in my pajamas, hanging the last of my duds in the closet when he returned, knocking lightly on the door. Ernie stood behind him, holding a small shot glass on a tray. He extended it to me. "Here. Drink hearty."

I looked at Glendon and he nodded, smiling. "It's our own secret brew. If you can manage to get it all down, believe me, it will take away your desire for liquor for at least twenty-four hours."

I took the glass and sniffed it. It was cloudy-looking and smelled awful. I took a deep breath and tilted my head and threw it all down.

I handed the glass back to Ernie and felt my knees buckle at the same time. I felt suddenly very hot and the room seemed to rock under my feet. I looked at Glendon and his expression seemed one of purely benign curiosity. Curse you, Red Baron, I wanted to say, but a slow-moving band of iron was clamping down hard inside my head. I found myself tilting forward very slowly. The room spun and the iron band inside my head exploded into a battery of rockets. They all went off, one by one, followed by a cascade of brilliant lights. The lights hurt my eyes and I had to close them. Everything inside me was going to sleep and it seemed to me a hell of a lot of trouble to go to instead of having a drink. I wanted to tell George Glendon about this, but my tongue felt a mile too thick and I knew as the last red rocket seared through my skull that I was in trouble.

When I opened my eyes, I was flat on my back. I tried to

raise my head but couldn't. I heard the soft gushing sound of voices. My vision cleared temporarily and I saw a chunky light-haired man standing next to Glendon. He wore light-rimmed eyeglasses and I knew I had seen him before.

I knew his name was Dorn, but I couldn't figure what he was doing looking down at me. I tried to raise myself up to ask him, but there were solid straps of tight canvas lashing me securely to the bed. I didn't need anything more to tell me that once again I had miscalculated my moves, and underestimated theirs.

I shook my head and tried to growl and fell asleep instead. I was getting pretty good at that.

Eighteen

"He's coming around."

I couldn't place the voice but would have given him ten-to-five odds he was wrong. I felt strung out, disconnected, disembodied. There was buzzing in my ears. My head seemed big as a balloon and ready to pop. My eyelids were heavy and felt hinged by heavy weights. I made a supreme effort and got them open. My eyes were instantly stabbed by bright overhead lights boring down in triple layers of flickering colors. I closed them and felt better, but I still wanted to know where I was, and what was happening to me, and I opened them again.

I was on my back, tilted toward the ceiling. Square tiles shifted in and out of focus and finally settled into a pattern that held. I'd seen ceilings before and this one was nothing special. I tried to shift and roll over. Various unfriendly parts of my body pinched tightly and told me I couldn't.

A man in a white surgical gown walked toward me in three-quarter time. He came close and leaned forward. The starch in his uniform made fierce crackling noises. I tried lifting my hands to close my ears, but they were lashed behind me.

I was lying on a tilted narrow board barely wide enough for my frame. My feet rested on an angled slab at the bottom.

I recognized the contraption as the exercise slant board used in gyms, one you can tilt back or raise a number of degrees. It is padded, covered with leather, and the weight lifters do their curls and presses from whatever angle they prefer. I've been on them before but never with my arms pulled back behind the board and tied there. Apparently I was going to learn a new exercise.

My head felt much too heavy to raise, so I tried looking down past my nose. Straps bisected my body. My upper torso was stripped bare. Wires were strung along me at intervals, extending out of view. It was too early for Christmas and I tried getting up. Pain parted my scalp with a violent no-no. Phantom fingers of metal were telling me to lie there quietly, not to move.

The white gown swam into view again and I thought I could raise my legs and get at him with a scissors move. Tiny nerve endings in my thighs exploded and ripped through me like hot wires searching for the marrow of my bones. I lay still.

"He's ready now."

I wanted to laugh coarsely and tell him he was ridiculous. A machine hummed. A million volts of concentrated force hit me in the back. My body tensed and surged upward, tearing the breath out of me. I settled back, nerves quivering and jiggling, and waited for the next one. A strange smell filled my nostrils. I identified it immediately. The musky scent of fear. My cortex knew what my body didn't. That I was going to be tickled to death.

I remembered watching through the see-through mirror with that eminent spa director George Glendon as the man inside the spare white room writhed and buckled under the impact of that marvelous new electronic device known as the isotron. I could still hear Glendon's words. "There is no pain. His face is contorted because it's the body's natural reaction. His muscles are being contracted rhythmically at five-second impulses."

I also remembered feeling as I watched the subject flinch

and squirm that he was being killed before my eyes. Glendon had assured me there was no pain because the electrical impulses by-passed the body's motor nervous system. I knew he didn't know what he was talking about and felt the beads of fear and sweat form on my brow as I counted off the five seconds for the next stimulated impulse.

I was ready when it came, but it didn't help. My flesh twitched as the contact wire bit into it and I jumped. It wasn't any worse than being branded by a hot iron.

"Why are you here, Mr. Roper?"

I could have told him. Because I was a dumb dick.

Glendon's voice sounded again from behind me. "We're waiting for an answer."

It left me another second to come up with one. I passed and the isotron probed my left-shoulder-blade area. My entire upper left quadrant recoiled in a monstrous heave. Glendon was right about its benefits. I could have hurled the sixteen-pound shot left-handed for a new world record on that one teeny jab.

He came up close to my right shoulder. "I'm sure you understand your body and nerves will give out long before the machine. I'll ask you once more. Why are you here?"

I found my tongue, although it seemed heavier than usual. "I told you. To get in shape. Take some weight off."

He nodded impassively and signaled to the man in control of Dr. Caligari's magic cabinet. The contact pad on my left side passed some of the electricity from the wire into my nerves by way of the muscles. I tried not to respond and twitched like a harem hopeful in a shimmy contest. After my body settled back, there was more jangling and quivering inside. My autonomic nervous system was calling for a huddle, asking what the hell was going on.

Glendon repeated his question. I gave him my answer. The isotron delivered its voltage. My body contorted and leaped, jiggled and contracted. In between shots, I was doing what came naturally to a bowl of jello, my nervous system exploding in long undulating ripples. I shivered and shook uncontrollably. Each contact stimulated another mass of ganglia into a palsied reflex. I expected any moment a contraction severe enough to snap a bone. I listened for the crack but heard only the sound of my grunts and panting and the soft humming of the isotron.

The man in the white gown came back into focus. I recalled his name. Dr. Savage. It didn't do much good. I was as helpless as a brand-new air-mail stamp under the register at the post office.

"It's twenty minutes," the doc said tonelessly. "Any more would be dangerous for the first treatment."

I could have told him that portion of my brain called the medulla oblongata had already passed along the message to all my nerve endings. "His reflexes are being overstimulated by repetition," the doc said. "He'll be into spasm soon."

Glendon thought it over.

"What the hell's going on?" I asked. "Do you treat all your customers this way?"

Glendon leaned over me. "You're a phony, Roper. You're no more in the insurance business than I am."

I remembered Dorn. He had found out I wasn't an attorney, either. I couldn't figure why he had to reveal my compulsive urge for new identities to Glendon. "It's a new line," I said. "I'm just learning the ropes."

"You're a liar," he said. "You're a private investigator. You're stripped now and even Dr. Savage is impressed with your musculature. If there's any surplus fat on you, it's all between your ears."

The observation about my physique rekindled my spirit. I thought I had become a marshmallow. I wasn't hurt any by his remark about my fat head. It was a condition which, although never overly fond of, I had learned to live with.

Glendon tapped my chest. I twitched. I hoped Dr. Savage's explanation covered my reaction this time. Otherwise I would probably have to learn to sing and dance after I got out.

"I'm asking you once more. What are you looking for

here?" He surprised me by smiling. "It's safe for you to tell me. I assure you whatever it is will be forgotten by the time you go."

I tried to focus on his face. "If you think I'm keeping something back, why haven't you clowns thought of using Sodium Pentothal? That's supposed to be pretty good for finding out the truth. Why the muscle-bender treatment?"

"The isotron is more memorable to the user," Glendon said. "It might deter you from seeing us again. By the time we've done with you, rest assured it will be the most memorable experience of your life."

I shook my head. It hurt and a lot of strange new marbles I never knew I had rolled around and finally found corners to rest against. "You're wrong, sweetie-pie. What I'm going to do to you when I get out—that's the thing I'm going to remember. The best and the most."

Glendon sighed and drew his head back. He signaled the good doctor. "Let's have one more for the road for Mr. Roper."

It was a good one, but it didn't break my back.

Glendon stepped forward again and listened as I softly cursed him. "Yes," he said sympathetically. "I understand your feelings. However we'll try you again in a little while and perhaps you'll be more cooperative."

Dr. Savage came forward again. I saw the hypo in his hand and foolishly tried to draw away. The wires that held me in place resisted. My forearm was swabbed and the needle went in.

"You might like that one," Glendon said, purring. "It's PCP—the peace pill. Good for hallucinations, delusions and, possibly, a depressed state."

I swam in the sea of the drug and pitching waves of pain. Glendon had me back on the rack. His lips opened. Words came out on a colorful ribbon of sound. They looked beautiful as they floated around in the close, acrid-smelling room. The acrid taste was in my mouth, too.

"Why are you here? What do you want? What are you looking for?"

He phrased the questions at five-second intervals as I recoiled and bucketed into endless contractions, an unwilling but jerking puppet to the repetitive voltage of the isotron. Tiny polliwogs flipped and did somersaults up and down my spinal column.

"I told you. Weight problem."

A million ants and grasshoppers were doing a war dance across my body down to my groin. My legs and arms ached and seemed on fire. The entire network of my agitated nerve endings was exploding, screaming for relief. I knew the muscle contractions were piling up a heavy oxygen debt. Lactic acid was building up, the end result of nerve impulse and motor action. Flooding of the molecules in the muscle tissue causes the muscle fiber to swell. Contractions compress the capillaries, squeezing the blood from them into the veins. I was drowning in my own fluids. An enormous engorged insect threatening to burst.

I jerked as the contact pads fed me another big jolt. My legs exploded and seemed torn apart. My toes twitched. I rolled my ankles to rub them. I realized suddenly the last contraction had snapped the bands lashing my legs to the oblique board.

I moaned. I made gurgling noises in my throat.

The white-coated Dr. Savage came over. He was holding a stethoscope, his face curiously impassive, free from diabolic glee. I respected a man dedicated to the pursuits of science and the improvement of his craft, involved in the pure aesthetics of his profession. I waited until he was close. I hooked my right foot between his thighs under his groin and drew him closer. Major inner reaping. *Ouchi-gari*. My left foot kicked out toward his groin, striking sharply with the instep. *Kin-geri*. Dr. Savage gasped and fell forward. My left heel continued upward, kicking violently with a twist. *Kakato-geri*. His head snapped back, he groaned, and fell on me.

Glendon came rushing over. He was a step away when I let the doctor drop and hooked him in with my right foot. Minor inner reaping. *Kouchi-gari.* He didn't know my legs were free and his mouth opened in surprise. I shut it with an ankle kick. *Kansetsu-geri.* Then I punished him with a round-house kick to the neck. *Mawashi-kubi-geri.* Side kick to the abdomen. *Yoko-geri.* Another of the same to the chin and he fell forward gasping.

I got both legs around him and squeezed hard. Triangle neck-lock. *Sankaku-jime.* His eyes bulged and he turned red.

"Cut me loose or I'll kill you," I said.

I squeezed harder, making his eyes pop. Then I jerked him forward and he sprawled on me. I shifted my legs to his waist. It was an ordinary leg-scissors now, but he knew I could strangle him to death that way as well as any other. I released him long enough for him to drop his hands across my body. He winced as I added more pressure and I felt him getting my hands and arms free.

I let him droop on my body a little longer, trusting him to remember we were not meant to be lovers. "Now take off the contact pads."

My hands were still palsied when they came free. It was difficult to make a fist. I gave him wrist (*koken*), palm heel (*shotei*), and sword-peak hand (*toho*). He went down and I sat up.

The door opened and Ernie the husky light-haired guard and male nurse walked in. He was carrying another of those wicked little shot glasses on a tray. He saw me sitting, rocking back and forth, trying to stop all those twitching little muscles that didn't know yet that fun time was over. His head cocked in surprise and then he saw Glendon and the doc on the floor. He set the tray down and came charging over.

I waited and timed it with a perfect high kick (*keage*), catching him flush on the jaw with the ball of my foot. He buckled forward. I gave him the inverted-fist strike to the spleen (*uraken hizo-uchi*) and he turned green. Inner knife-hand (*haito*) followed by knife-hand (*shuto*) toppled him like a chopped tree.

I got to my feet and allowed myself to twitch and jerk like an accomplished dipso after a three-month binge. The spasms ended and I leaned over and pulled Glendon up. The keys to my clothing locker were in his pocket. I got them out and shook him awake. "Where's Pam Clayton?" I asked for openers.

He shook his head. "I . . . don't . . . know."

I slammed him down on the slant board on which I'd recently been practicing fits. I strapped him tightly and reached for the tentacled contact pads. "Where's Clayton's kid?"

Reason returned to his eyes, widening into fear. "She isn't here. We let her go."

"What's it all about? Why hold her and cover up her appointment?" He hesitated and I showed him the contact pads.

"It wasn't my idea. I had to—"

"Who's behind it? Who gave you the orders?"

His eyes rolled sideways. I picked up the movement of the blond male nurse Ernie on the floor. "Don't go away," I told Glendon. I picked Ernie's potent little shot glass off the tray and showed it to him. "Drink hearty." He gagged, swallowed, and fell back into slumberland. Doc Savage was still unconscious, breathing heavily.

When I returned to Glendon, he was beginning to tremble. Beginning to react before the current prodded him.

I let him sweat out his fear a moment more. "Before I blacked out, I saw a man in my room with you. His name is Dorn. He works for Louis Charnock. Tell me, Glendon, does he have a piece of your action here?"

He hesitated, licked his lips. "N-no. He happened to be in the neighborhood. We—we know each other slightly."

"Come off it," I told him. "You admitted snatching Pam

Clayton wasn't your own idea. Those questions you were asking me sounded like you were fronting for a bigger fish. Who was it?"

He was playing a pantomime that reminded me of an old song, his lips telling me no, no, while there was yes, yes in his eyes. "Mr. Dorn suggested it," he said finally. "He didn't explain his plan to me. I—I had to do it."

"Why? You've got yourself a pretty good job here. How come you have to take orders from Charnock and Dorn?" I had a glimmer about their kind of operation. "Don't tell me you've been careless, Glendon. Have they got something on you? Some little boo-boo you've made you'd rather not get blown about?"

He gnawed helplessly at his lip.

"Is that it? Either you cooperate or he blows the whistle on you?"

He nodded, sweating.

Expensive out-of-town spas like the Gilded Cuckoo had wealthy patrons. Whatever their hang-ups, booze, drugs or sex, Glendon in his capacity as director would know them. He would know their financial ratings, too. It put him in a choice position for practicing blackmail. If Charnock had any kind of hold on him, he and Dorn could use the contacts and apply a lot of leverage. Glendon's setup was the kind I imagined would appeal to an old pro like Louis Charnock and his capable aide Dorn.

Still, Glendon could be conning me. The racket idea his own. Calling on Charnock and Dorn for outside professional help and splitting down the middle with them. Fear of the isotron rack was perhaps persuading him to agree to any question. My own nerves and muscles still twitched involuntarily, a reminder of the ordeal it could be. Torquemada could have doubled his fun with it. If the Women's Libbers had it, it would be over for us all.

Although I had supposed Dorn to be working for Charnock, he had seemed formidable enough at our first meeting to impress me into thinking he was capable of doing some moonlighting on his own. "You're saying Dorn. Do you mean Louis Charnock? Is he the big wheel giving the orders?"

Glendon twitched, nodding. "Y-yes."

I wondered. "Okay, you had the Clayton kid doped up. What then? A set of compromising pictures to make her old man cough up a lot of loot?"

"No. Nothing like that," he said hoarsely. "She was given sedation. To keep her quiet. That was all."

"What was the next step to be—a ransom note to Clayton?"

"I . . . don't know. The next day Mr. Dorn told me to release her."

"What scared him off? Was it too hot after Willie Rich was found drowned in his pool?"

"I don't know. Perhaps—but Mr. Dorn didn't say."

"Do you know who killed Willie Rich?"

"No." He saw me glance impatiently toward the isotron panel box. "I swear I don't know anything about that."

"Maybe," I said. "Getting back to Clayton's kid, you say Dorn told you to hold her. Was the hairdresser in on it?"

"No. When she arrived, I told her there was a personal phone call for her in my office. I offered her a drink while she was waiting for the switchboard to connect her. It contained the drug and put her out almost immediately. We then placed her in a private room. She was kept under sedation meanwhile."

"Twenty-four hours?"

"Approximately, yes."

"How did you explain it to her when she recovered?"

"We had one of our staff doctors handle it. He told her she had fainted. That there was some new mysterious twenty-four-hour virus going around. She didn't argue about it. She took what he said rather submissively, and left."

"Did she ask if you had notified her family?"

"No."

"It might interest you to know she hasn't returned home yet. Was she driving her own car when she left?"

"Yes. The green Mustang."

"Did she say anything about leaving for Lake Tahoe?"

"Not a word. I assumed she would be going home directly."

"You assume rotten. Miss Clayton wasn't your only client with a lot of money behind her. Why was she picked?"

"I—I don't know."

"Why that particular day—Labor Day?"

"I don't know. Mr. Dorn saw the appointment book—" He stopped, flustered.

"It's all right, Glendon. I know you phonied it up. It probably wasn't the first time you've had to improvise with a client's appointment. I hope you've made a lot of money, because you're going to need it for a good lawyer."

He shivered.

"What about Tom Hunter?"

His jowls quivered and he blinked more than he had to.

"Hold it a second," I said. "I think Doc Savage turned the current off."

He was screaming before I took two steps. "H-he's inside. L-last room. Ground floor. N-number eleven."

"What have you got him in for?" He hesitated and I leaned closer. "After what you gave me, I can leave you wrapped up in this machine until your muscles pop out of your skin. Talk!"

He was shaking, teeth chattering. "Hunter suspected we had Miss Clayton here. He started to take the place apart. We had to jump him. Quiet him down."

"Okay. You also told me you let the girl go. Why not do the same for Hunter?"

His face was white. "Again—I was ordered not to. They were afraid he'd make trouble."

"Who—Charnock and Dorn?" He nodded weakly. "Who the hell is this guy Hunter anyway?"

"I don't know."

"Okay. We'll find out. What were you doing to him meanwhile?"

His tongue flicked to wet his lips. "M-memory block," he said hoarsely. "We were trying to erase his memory."

I glanced at the isotron. "With this damn gadget?"

"N-no. Drugs and hypnosis. Conditioned regression."

I unbuckled his strap. "Let's go."

It was beddie-bye time at the Cuckoo. The corridors were quiet. From behind the closed doors of the live-ins, I heard contented giggles. Apparently, favors were reserved for certain visitors. I glanced at George Glendon, but he was too concerned with the new low estate of his own affairs to explain the leak in his security system. Ernie had probably put my confiscated fifth of Scotch to some good use, after all.

We found the room I had been assigned. I had Glendon wait in the closet until I was dressed. My bag hadn't been gone over thoroughly and my gun was still in its secret compartment. I nudged Glendon with it. "Time to check out the mystery guest."

He nodded politely and I followed him to the room at the end of the corridor. He unlocked the door and I waved him in. A man was lying on the bed, staring listlessly at the ceiling. His face was pale and haggard, eyes rimmed with dark circles. A wide gauze bandage topped his skull.

He didn't know he had visitors. I tapped Glendon's arm. "What's under the bandage—a small hole bored in his skull? Electrode implants for altering behavior?"

Glendon glanced at me impatiently, giving me no credit for my familiarity with the latest in scientific miracles. "It's nothing like that at all. He put up a fight and banged his head falling. A very mild concussion, at the worst."

"What about the drug treatment and the hypnosis you mentioned? How much of his memory have you erased?"

Glendon said petulantly, "He hasn't responded to hypnosis at all. There are some like that, you know."

"Tough," I said. I waved my hand and the man on the bed ignored it. "Maybe you know what's wrong with him?"

"Merely the effect of the narcotics," said Glendon. "All

it's done has been to put him in a stupor. It will wear off in a day or so. I assure you he'll be quite all right."

I leaned over the bed. "Mr. Hunter?"

He stared at the ceiling another moment, then shifted his eyes and found mine. He stared without comprehension. I pulled Glendon forward. "Say something," I told him. "Maybe you did better than you want me to think."

Glendon cleared his throat and snapped his fingers. "How are you tonight, Mr. Hunter?"

The man shifted his gaze to the spa director. A spark of anger glinted in his eyes. Apparently, for a change, Glendon had told me the truth.

"Is your name Hunter?" I asked. "Tom Hunter?"

He thought about it. "That's me," he croaked hoarsely. "Who the hell are you?" He spoke slowly with a softly slurred Spanish accent.

"I'm a friend of Willie's," I said. "Willie Rich."

Glendon glanced at me. "So that's it."

"That's part of it," I said. "Let's get Hunter dressed. I'm taking him along with me."

Mentioning Willie's name didn't bring about any response in Hunter. He resumed his concentrated stare at the ceiling, ignoring Glendon and me. We got him to sit up and hoisted him into his clothes. He remained passive until we stood him on his feet. He balked suddenly, hunching his shoulders, balling his fists.

His eyes glinted angrily. "Hold on a minute. I'm not leaving without the kid." He looked surprisingly alert suddenly.

"Pam Clayton's not here," I said. "Take my word for it."

He swung around, swaying like a drunk. "Why the hell should I?" he demanded. "Who the hell are you?"

"I told you before," I said. "A friend of Willie's. Pam's left. We're going too, pal. Come on."

He brushed my hand off his arm. His fingers weren't any harder than a pair of pliers. "Where'd she go?"

Glendon shook off my inquiring glance. "I swear I don't

know, Mr. Hunter. But I can assure you she's gone. She's probably home with her family by now." He looked at his watch, then at me. "You'd better hurry. The night shift will be coming on soon. I'd rather not be seen . . . this way. It's rather irregular." He made helpless waving motions with his hands.

He seemed apprehensive and I saw no point to running into more guards. I pulled Hunter out of his room. He looked back at it and waved. *"Poso del mundo,"* he muttered. Idiomatic for the lowest hole in the world.

Glendon heard and flushed. Considering his various sidelines, he was quite sensitive. Hunter's eyes had closed. He was asleep on his feet.

It was a short walk down the hall to the side exit. As we hit the cool night air, Hunter's legs buckled and he went limp. Glendon assisted while I shoved him into my car. He seemed agitated, glancing about nervously. "Don't worry about it," I told him. "I'll explain it all to Charnock and Dorn when I catch up with them. Besides, you've a bigger worry, Glendon. Something you really should be nervous about. Who killed Bonnie Burns?"

He rocked back jerkily. "What? Are you joking—?"

"I found her up at Lake Tahoe with a knife in her back. Didn't they tell you that was the next step after you told her to start her vacation?"

He stared at me stupidly, licking his lips.

"You're being played for a patsy, Glendon. You can get ten to twenty as an accessory. Who told you to let Bonnie off?"

I heard a rustle behind us in the dark shrubbery separating the parking lots. Something whistled, glittering in the night. It thudded heavily close to me. Glendon's mouth opened in a surprised scream aborted suddenly as he coughed and fell against me. I judged the knife in his back to have at least a six-inch blade.

He was sagging, pulling my arms down with him and I couldn't find my gun. Behind the shrubbery a door slammed and an engine revved up. A car took off, careening wildly, tires screeching. It bucketed off, burning rubber. It was almost out of sight and traveling faster than I could think when its headlights came on.

Glendon was coughing frothy red bubbles, staring at me accusingly as if I'd asked him one question too many.

Nineteen

Allie Riegel opened his door. I crooked my index finger and backed off. He followed me down his driveway to my car, and stopped, puzzled, when I pointed inside. "What is it?" he asked.

"It's a Tom Hunter," I said. "Have you ever seen one?"

He peered inside and apparently he hadn't. "What is he—drunk?"

"Sleeping off a few days of a drug program at the Gilded Cuckoo. I just got him out."

Allie looked back at me more puzzled than before. "Why bring him here to me?"

"You're the first person I thought of."

"That's very nice. But doesn't he have a home?"

"It's too far away. Acapulco."

"I mean—here."

"He was staying at the Rover House. I thought he'd be safer here with you."

Allie shrugged. "Is he a friend of yours?"

"No. But he knew Willie Rich."

"I can think of about fifty thousand others who did, too," Allie said. "I appreciate your bringing only one."

"I thought we were interested in finding out who killed Willie, and why," I said.

Allie nodded. "Sure. What does this guy have to do with it?"

"I don't know. He's been in town a few weeks. Been trying to see Clayton. No dice. Clayton won't see him. He's been trying to call Clayton's kid, Pam. Clayton won't let her take the call. He leaves a message for her to call him. She never gets it."

"Clayton doesn't allow messages either?"

"Maybe Monica ixnayed that one."

Allie peered intently at the sleeping gent on the seat in my car. "Did I ask yet what's it got to do with Willie?"

"Maybe when he wakes up, he'll tell us. Meanwhile, all I have is secondhand. He wanted to see Pam Clayton. Apparently Willie set it up. I'm not sure yet if they actually did meet or were about to. He had a date to meet her at the track Labor Day. Clayton's kid had an appointment with the hairdresser at the Gilded Cuckoo and forgot to tell Hunter."

Allie looked at me. "You feeling all right?"

I put up my hand. "It gets better. Willie felt bad, for some reason, that she wouldn't be able to meet Hunter at Del Mar track. He came down to tell Joey Zale to give Hunter the message."

"I like mysteries," Allie said. "What message?"

"That she wouldn't be able to meet him at the selected time because she would be in Poway instead getting her hair fixed at the Gilded Cuckoo."

"You don't tell me."

"That's the way I heard it from Joey Zale."

"Okay," Allie said. "So instead he meets the kid at the Gilded Cuckoo. Right?"

"Wrong. But you like mysteries, so keep listening. He never got to see Clayton's kid at the Cuckoo because she had been previously abducted, or waylaid, drugged, and put into a private room there. Remember, she was missing?"

Allie scratched his head. "I never thought she was *that* missing."

"But she's not any more, because they let her go the next

day. That is, according to George Glendon, the spa director, they did."

Allie frowned. "Give me that name again. I'd like to have a few nasty words with him."

"You can't. Somebody threw a knife in him. He's dead."

Allie whistled.

"Hunter knew or thought he knew the kid was in there. Her appointment was for ten-thirty and supposedly he got there about then. He made a big stink when they tried to con him, saying she wasn't there. He suspected something was wrong, broke inside. They had to knock him out."

"What'd they use on him, for Christ's sake, a sledge hammer?" Allie yelped. "You mean he's been out since Labor Day? That was four days ago."

"Since then, according to Glendon while he was still well enough to talk, they've been using drugs on him and applied hypnosis."

Allie's jaw sagged. "What the hell for?"

"Conditioned regression, Glendon said."

"I'll stay with what I said before. What the hell for?"

"That's part of the mystery," I said. "Maybe it's because he knew Pam Clayton was there, being held against her will. Maybe they had a big kidnap and ransom caper planned and didn't want him to remember what he knew."

"Maybe," Allie said cautiously. "I'm surprised they went to all that trouble, if that was their game. Why didn't they just knock him off—kill him instead?"

"They had already done that with somebody else. A cute little receptionist who worked there the morning Pam Clayton walked in. They got her up in Lake Tahoe—also with a knife in her back."

"How did they get their receptionist up to Tahoe?"

"They remembered she had a vacation coming. When she came back after lunch, Glendon told her to take off, business was slow, they could spare her. At that point, they already had Hunter and the Clayton girl on ice."

"What changed their minds about holding on to Pam Clayton? You said they let her go."

"Glendon didn't know for sure. Said he was taking orders from somebody higher up."

"Who?"

"Fellow named Louis Charnock."

"When did they let her go?"

"The next day, he said. Approximately twenty-four hours."

Allie laughed mirthlessly. "That's a crock. She hasn't turned up home yet. I think you let Glendon pull your leg."

"That wasn't all he pulled." He looked interested and I gave him all the gory details. He still looked interested, so I added, "That's why I'm leaving Hunter with you tonight. I've got to get back up to L.A. to grab on to Dorn and Charnock."

"You didn't mention Dorn before."

I told him what I knew of the Charnock-Dorn relationship.

"They were wise to you back in their penthouse suite when you tried to come on as the attorney?"

I admitted they were.

"And they knocked you out today when you came back to the spa pretending you wanted to be a live-in taking the health course?"

I admitted they did.

"That's twice out of two they've nailed you. What makes you think you're going to do any better this time?"

"I might get lucky."

"You might also get your brains scrambled."

I got the car door open. "Let's get Hunter into your house first, and I'll be on my way."

We tugged at the lanky sleeping man and got him out of the car. With Allie leading the way, we brought him into the house.

"On the couch," Allie said. "He can sleep it off there."

We dumped him down without interrupting his sleep or

steady breathing. As I straightened up, I knocked a magazine off the low table. I picked it up. It was a local flyer, circulating in the San Diego area, listing things to do, places to go. A page fell open headed "Calendar of Coming Events." I stared.

Allie must have caught my expression. "Anything wrong?"

I shook my head, pointing to the column. The Plaza, a local theater in San Diego, was listed where for this night and the next two following, Louis Charnock, metaphysician of the twentieth century, would be giving his lecture series to the public. At no charge.

"It's a break," I said. "That's a ten-minute ride instead of the two-hour hop up to L.A. I'm glad you're so current-event-minded."

"Me, too," Allie said. "That's the first time I ever looked inside it." He glanced down at Hunter. "We can leave this guy here, you know. Maybe I can tag along with you. You might need some help with Dorn and Charnock."

I shook my head. "No, thanks. It's more important you keep Hunter alive till I get back. I don't know if there's a connection, but Monica Moore's first husband was a Hunter, too. Jeff Hunter."

"What's keeping him alive got to do with that connection?"

"I remember Jeff Hunter died suddenly a few months after they were married. The circumstances, I heard, were questionable. Maybe mysterious. Overdose of barbiturates."

Allie frowned, looked down at Hunter. "How long ago was this?"

"Fifteen, twenty years."

"You think they were brothers?" he asked.

"Could be. You'll know when he wakes up."

"Sure," Allie said, "but I was thinking of what you said before. That conditioned regression bit, blocking out his memory. What if you're wrong about that? What if they're trying to wipe out something else? Something that goes back fifteen or twenty years. Like his brother's murder, let's say?"

"No sweat," I said. "I'll ask Charnock about that when I see him."

Twenty

The drive down the freeway south to the San Diego theater took the best part of fifteen minutes. It was enough time to cool my thinking. I began to wonder what I really had on Louis Charnock apart from a natural dislike for a mountebank coming on as a saintly figure. I imagined his feeling for the buck was behind his polished mellifluous tones, but there could have been more behind it. Apart from my seeing Dorn in my room at the Cuckoo while under the effects of the drug they had slipped me, I had only Glendon's word for his involvement. I couldn't forget that he was in fear of his life then, inclined to go along with anything I suggested to get off the rack. I had built up the whole picture out of surmise, conjecture and one slight glimpse of Charnock's associate Dorn. The more I thought of it, the less I liked what I had on him. Charnock had been in the self-appointed Messiah business too long, built up too big and loyal a following, to let himself get involved in the shady machinations I had him backing at the Gilded Cuckoo health and beauty spa.

The Plaza theater was on G Street, just off the hotel circle in downtown San Diego. It was late when I parked, the doors closed, Charnock's lecture apparently well under way. I saw his black Lincoln parked on the side street, the burly chauffeur nowhere in sight. The ticket office was closed and I drifted past, hearing the slight patter of applause. I figured it would take another ten to fifteen minutes before Charnock finished, giving me time to plan a careful and circumspect approach when I braced him. I had a lot of questions to ask about his operation and I couldn't afford the errors I had made on my previous attempt.

The alley near the theater was dark and quiet. I stepped into it, striking a lighter to a cigarette. As I inhaled, a dim bulky form materialized out of the darkness. A hand grabbed my lapel while another, bunched and no harder than a rock, crashed against the side of my jaw.

Rockets sputtered inside my head. I staggered back against the brick wall of the theater dazed, knowing I was in big trouble. A pile-driving blow to the pit of my stomach took my breath away. My knees buckled. A wave of nausea flooded over me and suddenly I was through. As I sagged helplessly, I saw his face for the first time. He looked happy and I couldn't blame him. It was the burly blond chauffeur in Charnock's employ, the playmate called Jay Jay.

"We decided to finish up sometime, remember?" he said.

He didn't wait for an answer, clubbed me behind the ear, and it was all over. As I went down, all those sputtering rockets looping around inside my skull went out one by one. Darkness enveloped me, dragging me down and down, until I couldn't fall any farther. I knew I was dead and there wasn't a single thing I could do about it.

I smelled the dank alley first, then the cool night air. My eyes opened and I heaved and gulped and groaned and got up. Jay Jay was gone and I had the alley all to myself. I was sick of it and reeled along the wall until I could walk out of it.

There was a thin cluster of people chatting on the walk in front of the theater. The lobby lights were out, cars were driving away into the distance. I limped around the corner to my car, got it going, and drove slowly around the block. Lady Luck, guiltless as ever and smiling, wafted gently beside me, blowing me a kiss. I heard voices and doors slam. I stopped my heap abruptly, staring happily as I saw Louis Charnock, in white as ever, step into his long black car. The other man, Dorn, wasn't with him. The bulky beetled blond chauffeur was good enough for me. He let Charnock in, slid behind the wheel, and drove off. I gave him half a block and followed.

He turned down toward the Embarcadero, drove north along the waterfront. The Navy ships were ghostly gray and quiet, long guns covered against the fog. The glittering restaurants along Harbor Drive reminded me I was hungry. There were plenty of hotels in San Diego, but Charnock was heading north out of the city.

We skirted the yacht harbors of Coronado Island, and I tailed him up Highway 101 to Midway Drive, to Mission Bay. This is the new vacationland for the tourists and Charnock had become one. His driver swung off the causeway where a curving ramp led to a supersumptuous motor hotel. Its lights told me it was the Bahia Bay. A NO VACANCY neon told me business was good. I didn't want a room so much as a resolution.

The black car pulled into a parking stall at the far end, fronting a dark bungalow. I stopped, put out my lights, saw Charnock get out. He said good night to the chauffeur, opened a door, and went inside. Jay Jay lit a cigarette, leaned back against his seat, and enjoyed the quiet night.

His hand holding the butt dangled outside the open car window when I came up. I slammed his wrist to the side of the car, pinning it there, curling his fingers in tight so the burning butt could heat them up. He started to yell his surprise and I leaned in with a solid left, smashing his nose, aborting his outcry. I slugged him again, yanked the door open, pulled him toward me, and smashed him back flat on the seat. One good thing about the bloodletting business is it never hurts to have a sucker off guard.

I wanted Jay Jay out of the way fast. He was flat on his back and I went headlong in after him. *Shime waza* covers most strangling techniques, with neck-locks standard. Crossing my forearms in front of Jay Jay's throat, I gripped each side of his collar, one hand with the thumb inside his jacket, the other with the fingers inside. It's called the half-cross neck-lock (*kata-juji-jime*), the arms and wrists operating as scissors, the wrists as the blades, the elbows as the handles. It cuts off blood circulating to the brain. Jay Jay went limp in a few minutes. I removed his belt, lashed his hands behind him, and dumped him back over the front seat. He hit the floor of the rear section with his head and gave a pretty good imitation of a dead bodyguard.

Charnock opened his bungalow door when I knocked. His eyes had a questioning look. They changed expression when I showed my gun. He backed up fast and I shut the door behind me, locking it. "I had a lot of questions to ask you last time we met," I told him. "We never got into them. Now I have several more. Let's start with George Glendon. What's your connection with him?"

His thick jet eyebrows flew up and stayed there. "George who?"

He looked as blank after I repeated Glendon's name. "He runs the health and beauty spa at Poway. The Gilded Cuckoo. He also seems to have been running a lot of errands for you."

Charnock shook his head and gave his eyebrows a rest. "I'm sorry—Mr. Roper, isn't it?—I don't know either the gentleman or what you're talking about."

"How about Pam Clayton? Does that ring a bell?"

Again the blank stare and slight negative head shake. "I don't know her. I know Monica Clayton, of course. But then, we've known each other for many years."

I looked down at the gun in my hand, realizing suddenly that Charnock was showing absolutely no fear. His sonorous voice was hitting all the usual decibels, and if it had any tremor, I wasn't able to detect it. "This gun can go off," I reminded him. "A little while ago, your chauffeur racked me up pretty good in the alley outside the San Diego theater while you were giving your lecture. I was also given a pretty good going over at the Gilded Cuckoo by the same Mr. Glendon I mentioned earlier. Don't tell me you don't know anything about it, because I've heard a different story. Also I happened to see your associate Dorn there at the time."

A light flickered in Charnock's eyes. "Oh," he said mildly, "that's quite possible. Mr. Dorn might have some interest there. He has many outside interests, you see. None of them concern me."

"Let's try two other names, Charnock. Bonnie Burns. Tom Hunter."

"I'm sorry. I don't know them."

"Does Dorn?"

He shrugged. "It's quite possible. I suggest you ask him."

"I will when I get to him. But he works with you and until I'm convinced otherwise, you're implicated in what's happened. Pam Clayton was abducted, held prisoner at the spa. So was Hunter. Bonnie Burns, a receptionist, was killed. So was Glendon."

He registered a demisemiquaver of shocked silence. Then, "I don't know any of them. I don't know anything about any of it."

I wagged the gun impatiently. "You may have a faulty memory."

He shook his head. "On the contrary. My memory is perfectly sound. I don't know those people."

I unflipped my wallet and showed him the buzzer. "I'm a private investigator, Charnock. On Labor Day, Willie Rich, a good jockey and friend of mine, was drowned in his swimming pool. I don't think it was his idea, and I'm trying to find out who killed him, and why. I think you're somehow involved.

"Tyler Clayton's daughter was reported missing the morning of the same day. Monica Clayton asked me to find her. The girl had a beauty appointment at the spa. Glendon told me she never got there. Subsequently he admitted drugging her, keeping her a prisoner there. He said he was acting on orders from higher-ups, and implicated you and Dorn.

"Monica Clayton called on you the following day in Los

Angeles. I saw her come into the theater to your lecture, later in your car. Why? Are you still giving her spiritual guidance? Or was she there to discuss a possible ransom transaction between you and Tyler Clayton for his daughter?"

Sad dark eyes glittered in his pale face. "I gave her no guidance of any kind. She didn't come to see me. She came to see Dorn."

I slapped my knee. "Maybe you can tell me why."

"I imagine," he said, "to bring him some money."

"Money? What for?"

"The usual reason, I suppose. Blackmail."

I looked at him.

"It's been going on for a long time," he said. "A good many years."

"That's great," I said. "A nice clean operation. Is that how you always manage to get your donations—using Dorn as your front man?"

His rich deep voice was softly demurring. "It's not quite as you think. It's the other way around really. Mr. Dorn uses me as *his* front. I happen to be a convenience to suit his own purposes."

I stared, remembering the incident after I had been ejected from their suite. The harsh name-calling after the door to Charnock's study was closed, Dorn reaming him out. The slap and almost simultaneous gasp of pain. I had assumed Dorn to be on the receiving end for overstepping his bounds. "The day I called," I said, "Dorn slapped *you?*"

"Possibly if I explained our relationship," Charnock said, "you might understand."

Twenty-five years ago Charnock had committed an indiscretion. It was with a minor, a male, good for a morals rap. Wesley Dorn, a sharp and conniving lawyer, got the evidence, and found himself in a position to put an end to young Charnock's platform career. But he was shrewd enough to sense a better arrangement.

A partnership, instead, with Dorn calling the shots.

"I was young then," Charnock continued. "Inexperi-

154

enced. Terrified by Dorn's threats. I have always been easily intimidated."

It might have been a cursory bluff, but a clever con man like Dorn would know how to press his advantage. Sensing the susceptibility of his pigeon, Dorn had moved in and taken over, making a lifetime arrangement as a living latch-on in a growing concern.

Charnock had been a success from the start. Women had been smitten with his looks, his boyish charm, his voice. They flocked to his lectures like lemmings to their last big night out on the beach. They filled the halls, bought up his books, enrolled for his courses. They fought for his favors, not realizing he had none to give.

"They gave me money," he was saying. "Large amounts. They remembered me in their wills. They've given me real estate, businesses, insurance policies. Incredible, really."

"But you never got a dime out of it?"

He smiled. "You might say living expenses."

Dorn had secured Charnock's power of attorney. The donations and inheritances, the wealth passed directly into his hands. The contacts were all Charnock's, but Dorn made them his own. He got the women he wanted out of it, too. Charnock's operation was a golden goose constantly renewing itself as he did his tours and wrote his books. Dorn meanwhile played his part as submissive aide to the master in public cleverly. Nobody suspected that when the platform lights went out, the relationship changed hands and Dorn took over. He had parlayed a minor felony into a fortune.

"You could have got out," I said. "Dorn didn't make you write your books with a gun to your head. You could have come up with a sore throat at some of your lectures. You're putting a lot into your work. You don't sound like a prisoner."

"Don't misunderstand," he said. "I believe in my messages, my books, my lectures. I'm permitted to do what I like to do. Like it or not, Dorn has made it possible for me to continue my work. He's organized the program, made it work for us both. True, he's gotten what he's wanted out of it, but so have I. Despite his hold on me, I sincerely believe that I've helped a good many people. I don't think of being a prisoner to Dorn and my youthful folly any more. I've accepted it."

"Okay. You like your role onstage, and the idea that you're influencing people to better lives. You get the handshakes and the applause from the crowd. You're happy despite everything. It doesn't always work out that way. You told me Monica Clayton is paying off to Dorn, too. What's he got on her?"

"At the start of her career, to further it, I believe, she made some short films—for private consumption—that kind of entertainment."

"Stag movies? Party flicks?"

"Yes. Dorn managed to obtain some of the early prints."

"She buys them back and finds out he's developed new ones?"

"Yes."

It wasn't a new racket, but then it never had to be if you had the right kind of leverage.

"He's had her on the hook all these years?"

Charnock nodded. "He's been clever enough to make— uh—new arrangements. Monica has been rather careless, you might say, at different stages of her life. She's been unfortunate enough to have picked up some bad habits."

"Drugs?"

"That, too."

I had a better picture and understanding now of Goerge Glendon's spa operation. Monica had been a guest or visitor or patient many times before. The little red-headed receptionist Bonnie Burns had told me that much. She could have gone in for treatment, for a fix, for whatever she needed and could afford. Dorn, alert to any opportunity to keep her on the hook, had probably followed her there, made his alliance with Glendon. If he had made new arrangements, as Charnock suggested, they would be on the basis of any new habit she was living with, or trying to kick. Photos taken on the scene would be easy enough to manage. They could then be superimposed any way Dorn and Glendon decided, the porno setups used as a threat in her new marriage with the very wealthy Tyler Clayton. Monica had paid and paid the dues of a lifetime already. It was a surprise to me that she was still willing to accept so much harassment. She didn't look nearly that pliable and long-suffering, and I couldn't understand Dorn still being alive. Charnock was born to be a patsy and a saint. Not Monica.

I wondered now what had really brought her up to see Dorn the night after Willie had been drowned, the day after Tyler's only daughter had mysteriously disappeared after a visit to a place Monica knew but too well.

I interrupted Charnock's narrative again. "I understand Lance Kite, Monica's fourth husband, wasn't pleased with the financial arrangements when they broke up. That money ostensibly given to you went to Dorn again?"

A negligent shrug. "Yes."

"Kite was displeased enough to start a suit charging extortion. He later dropped the charges and the suit. What changed his mind?"

"You've met our chauffeur Jay Jay," Charnock said. "He's an ex-heavyweight champion of the Navy. He was discharged for beating up an officer, served a few years in the stockade, later drifted in and out of rackets. His specialty is enforcement and he's sadistic enough to enjoy his work."

"You're suggesting Dorn sent Jay Jay over to persuade Kite?"

"Yes. In our brief association, Jay Jay has managed to persuade a good many people to change their minds. Naturally Kite hasn't been the first to demand a more equitable accounting. As I said before, a good many women have endowed us more than generously with their worldly goods. In many instances, their spouses weren't as enthused over our good work. Jay Jay managed to convince them to . . . uh . . . accept the inevitable."

"As *you* have, Charnock. He sounds like one hell of a

good company man and all-around bodyguard. But I notice you've still kept him on as your personal chauffeur."

"Well, yes, but again I have no say in the matter. Dorn saw to that. He protects me from people, true, seeing to it nothing happens to prevent me from performing my duties."

"Why not?" I said testily. "You're the original golden goose."

"It's only good business," Charnock said softly. "Dorn is nothing if not a good businessman. Jay Jay is useful, too, in making certain that I don't get out of sight and possibly out of line. They're still concerned, you see. They're very careful about whom I'm with. Tonight is rather an exception. I wonder how—"

"I've got him all wrapped up in the back of your car," I said. "That's how. If I go along with what you've been telling me, he jumped me in the alley and laid me out for Dorn, not you?"

Charnock spread his soft white hands apart. "I've nothing to fear from you, Mr. Roper. Apparently, Wesley Dorn has."

" 'Apparently' is hardly the word, Mr. Charnock," I said, getting to my feet. "Where's Dorn now?"

Charnock extended a long languid finger toward the window. "He has a houseboat in the cove. Only a short distance off the pier. It's called the *Sea Serpent*. You can't miss it even at night. It's positively unique."

"So is Dorn."

He was staring down at his hands when I left, and I wondered if that was about as far as he generally looked.

Twenty-one

After leaving Charnock, I looked into the back of his car to see how Jay Jay was doing. He was gone. Apparently love of duty and a thick skull were more than equal to what I had laid on him. It didn't disappoint me so much as make me determined to hit him a lot harder next time.

I thought he'd be waiting for me down at the dark end of the pier. He wasn't, and I found a small boat with oars and not too much water sloshing around on the floorboards. I made like Captain Bligh and headed for a large gray shape with bright lights bobbing a few hundred yards out on the bay. Several other boats were at anchor nearby, but this was the only houseboat affair.

It was campy and attractive, a large two-story gingerbread Victorian scow. I made out the name *Sea Serpent* and tied up to the side and hauled my way up on deck. The deck was an extended front porch. There were shutters on the windows and potted plants. There was a front door and a living room covered with brilliant red carpeting. Dorn was lying on it, face up, a lot of it missing above the eyes. I was a little disappointed but not too surprised.

Two bullets had pinpointed in his forehead causing immediate death, a blood-spattered wall, and an end to a very long successful career as a leech and louse. I couldn't imagine anyone mourning his loss.

I followed the wall-to-wall red carpeting up the steps to the upper floor. It had two bedrooms and a bath, decorated with a flair like the rest of it to look more like a modern house than a boat. There were feminine things in one of the bedrooms, but the labels didn't tell me anything more than I knew before, that Dorn liked women.

Pam Clayton wasn't lying in a closet or slumped in the bathroom shower stall. There wasn't anything I could find there the least suggestive of her presence. I hoped to find her still alive somewhere, but I wouldn't have wagered any decent sum on it.

Dorn's room had been carefully picked apart. Not all of the desk drawers were tightly closed, and things had been tossed about in his clothing commode. Either Dorn had been hastily looking for something or his killer had.

Dorn couldn't have been dead over an hour. I eliminated Louis Charnock, the big chauffeur Jay Jay and myself as suspects, leaving the rest of the world to consider. I was kind of annoyed at George Glendon for dying too soon, as he would have made a very plausible killer, to my thinking.

I got back into the little boat, rowed to the pier, and found my car. I debated whether or not to tell Charnock the good news, deciding against it, as I was afraid I'd find him dead, too, if I called back, and I had enough murders I couldn't solve.

It was nearly midnight and I threaded my way north against the fog sweeping in off the Pacific. Trucks thundered by heading south past a lot of cautious drivers on the freeway. I got off the murky soup at Del Mar and drove to Allie Riegel's house, wondering if perhaps the sleepy caballero from Acapulco had snapped out of his stupor and could tell me something.

Riegel's car was gone from his carport. That told me a little and when I opened the front door I learned some more. Hunter wasn't on the couch any more. Allie Riegel was on the floor, flat on his face doing his own imitation of a sleeping man.

I turned him over and he groaned. His eyes opened, he got mine into focus, and he made a wry expression. "Did you get him?" he asked.

"Get who?"

"The man you laid off here. Hunter. I leaned over to check how he was. He was ready and decked me." He glanced at his wrist watch. "Christ! I wasn't out long. You must have passed him."

"If I did, I never recognized him. He was wearing your car."

Allie sat up angrily. "What?"

I helped him to his feet, a little surprised that Hunter had taken out Allie, a big man, so easily. I soothed his ruffled feelings by filling him in on my activities since I'd left. He looked a little happier hearing how the chauffeur Jay Jay had rung my bell in the alley. "Too bad," he said, "but you more or less knew you would be walking into something. They were wise to you. What the hell reason did Hunter have for hanging one on me?"

"Maybe we'll find out when we catch up to him."

I checked my watch against Allie's and there didn't seem time enough for Hunter to have caught up with Dorn to wipe him out. Neither Allie nor I had bothered checking him out for a weapon.

Allie read my mind. "I carry a thirty-two in the glove compartment of my car," he said. "In case I was asleep longer than I care to admit, what kind of weapon knocked Dorn out of the ball game?"

"It could have been a couple of thirty-twos or a couple of strong plinking twenty-twos."

"A twenty-two, for crying out loud," Allie said disgustedly, "that's a woman's gun."

I nodded. "I've heard a lot about Monica Clayton, but nobody yet told me she wasn't a woman."

Allie wrinkled his nose. "You figure she did Dorn?"

"I can't figure what's taken her so long."

"That's crazy," Allie said. "If what Charnock told you is the truth, she wouldn't have waited all these years to knock Dorn off. Why now—tonight?"

"Frankly, that's what bothers me, too. That's why I'm not taking her too seriously about it. I figure Dorn's killer had a lot to do with the others—starting with Willie. I suppose Monica could have drowned Willie. Maybe she had a reason. But I can't see her throwing a knife into the little redhead up at Tahoe, nor in Glendon, either. I also figure it's got to tie up somehow with Tyler's daughter's abduction at the spa, and Tom Hunter's. He seems to be the only one still around who might be able to give me some answers."

"Swell," Allie said. "And after he gives you yours, remember he owes me one."

"That's not too hard to figure, Allie. He seems a stubborn cuss who came up here to do a job and he doesn't like being kept from doing it."

"Sounds reasonable. All you have to do then is find him."

"Right," I said. "It's late and I'm kind of pooped. I'd better get started."

Allie had his hand on my shoulder before I got halfway to his door. "You don't have to solve everything tonight. They've half killed you already today. Knock it off. As I once heard, tomorrow is another day."

"Now might be better. I want Hunter alive."

Allie stared. "How the hell do you know where he is?"

"I don't," I said. "All I've got is an idea."

Twenty-two

Moonbeams etched their ghostly fingers through the foggy night as I eased into the humpbacked drive in Escondido. The stately white ranch house of Willie Rich was dark and quiet.

Nobody was floating in the swimming pool lit up by a pale-green glow. The front door was locked and I tried the side door off the terrace. It was late by ordinary standards, but I hoped Penny Rich was out swinging somewhere according to her custom.

The lock was susceptible to a little applied effort and I went inside carefully. The curtain fell in place behind me and I put my thin pencil torch to work and found my way through the living room to Willie's den and study.

Pictures of Willie with the world's celebrities festooned the walls, cups and trophy mugs were all over the tables and bookshelves. I already knew how popular Willie was, but I still had no idea why his house had been entered and ransacked twice recently. Making it a third couldn't hurt.

The desk dominated the room—French Empire, massive, with swelling curves. It drew me like a magnet. I opened drawers and searched, wondering what I was looking for.

The lock to the center drawer had been forced. It contained several old racing programs, a pair of binoculars, a few bottles of vitamins which wouldn't do Willie any more good, and a small key. The key fitted the lock to the drawer.

I pulled out the drawer and studied it. It was shallow, the ringed handles bronze and beautifully ornamented. I set it down on the desk, stooped and searched the center with my torch. I couldn't find anything and compounded that by losing my balance. As I teetered forward, my hand struck the wood. There was a slight click as the wood yielded, then sprang back.

I tugged at it gently and out it came, another drawer, a secret compartment right out of Napoleon's day. I exulted too soon. There wasn't a thing in it. I turned it over and found an old auction sticker pasted on the bottom. The glue had dried and I peeled it off and pocketed it, set the drawers back in place and straightened up.

My thin-beamed torch flickered over the walls searching for a combination safe. With the kind of big money Willie made, it would have been natural for him to stash large sums around. The attempts Allie had mentioned of breaking in could have been warranted by the simple quest for money.

Something bumped heavily outside, interrupting my reverie. Car lights swept the driveway and I was on my way out before I heard the door slam and footsteps on the gravel.

I went out the side terrace door I'd used before. As I closed it, I felt the thin edge of cold steel against my throat. There wasn't a thing I knew in karate to counter that feeling.

I didn't recognize the blade, but I knew the voice of Johnny Cashio, purring silkily, as reassuring as the soft hiss of a rattler. "Working overtime, pal? Let's march it around the other side to the swimming pool. I want a good look at you."

Itsutsu-no-kata is five formulas. Symbolic demonstrations of five natural phenomena on which the principle of judo has been based: positive and negative, inertia, centripetal and centrifugal forces, tidal wave and comet.

Remembering Cashio's reputation with a knife, I chose

inertia and went along. It was awkward walking with his bent arm encircling my throat, but it beat a slit jugular.

Penny Rich was waiting, looking lovely and blowzily stoned. A calculated expression of outrage struggled to make headway in the tangled network of her brain. "Well, will ya look who's here?" she said in that baby voice, slurred with too much booze. "If it ain't Willie's blip-blip friend. Big blip-blip private-eye man. Big blip four-alarm fake." She threw in a few other knowledgeable blippers that would have warmed my ears if Cashio's knife hadn't been hovering under them waiting for a false move.

Willie's big outdoor pool with its reflected lighting glowed a sickly green as the moon poked through the over-cast. I thought of his last living moments here at the end of Labor Day. Although small, Willie was strong above the waist, as most jocks are. It would have taken a powerful man to hold him under until he drowned. The kind of weapon Cashio held might have forced him into the water, but that or a gun would have been only a preliminary. They still had to hold him under for three or four minutes. Five to be abso-lutely sure.

I remembered Cashio calling on Penny the day after, cool in his special reptilian way, arrogantly assured. I couldn't see him coming back so soon afterward if he'd had a hand in it. Even gangsters like Johnny Cashio had their own code. The punctilio of the underworld emphasized the cere-mony of scrupulous politeness. I was convinced Cashio was not Willie's murderer. Meanwhile I still saw my own future in doubt. I erased Willie and thought about me.

Penny Rich confronted me, fists jammed on hips, beauti-ful legs triangulated for better balance. "Well, wise guy, what's your excuse for breaking in? It's still *my* house, you know. *I* still live here. I'm not going to sit still while every two-bit punk in the neighborhood breaks in whenever he feels like it. What're you doing here anyway? Willie's not home. He's dead."

Cashio's blade nibbled at an inch of my neck. "Answer the lady, pal."

"Willie isn't just dead. He was drowned. I'm looking for his killer."

Cashio laughed mockingly. "You gotta be kidding, pal. You expect to find him hiding inside the house maybe?"

I started to shake my head and stopped short of killing myself. "I heard the house has been broken into a few times since. I figured whoever killed Willie was still looking for something Willie had. I thought maybe I could find it."

"Find what?" Penny asked.

"I don't know," I said.

Cashio pressed his blade closer. "Try harder to remember."

Behind us in the darkness gravel crunched on the driveway. Johnny Cashio tensed warily, turning his head. I twisted away, striking sharply upward and outward with *seiken jodan-uke*, forefist upper block. As his knife hand was knocked aside, I got an outside *tensho* cover on his wrist. At the same time I struck hard at his temple with *shuto gammen-uchi*, knife-hand strike to face. He sagged. I grabbed his head, pulling it down, and gave him *hiza-geri*, knee kick, driving hard into his face, feeling his molars give.

Cashio groaned and the knife fell clattering on the stone terrace. I added *atemi-waza*, vital stroke technique. *Nukite*, spear hand, fingers stiffly extended straight out. The thrust was sharply upward to his abdomen. He collapsed at my feet. Penny screamed and fell into a deck chair sobbing.

I found his knife and looked him over. He looked pretty bad, but I might have looked even worse. I threw his knife into the pool and walked away.

I got into my car, turned the key, and stepped on the starter. The engine caught and a man leaned across from the other side pointing a gun through the open window. It just wasn't my night.

"Glad you could make it, Mr. Hunter," I told him. "I've been looking all over for you."

He nodded and slid in beside me, putting the big .32 dead on my ear. It was a little better than Johnny Cashio's knife at my throat, but not too much.

"I'll take what you found in there," he said.

Twenty-three

"What were you expecting?"

"Whatever you found."

I kept my hands on the wheel. "Frisk. I've got nothing."

He ran his hands over my pockets expertly, keeping the gun leveled on my skull. "I'll be damned," he said finally.

"Mind if we move the car? I think I left a sore loser back there."

"Suit yourself. You might have another one here."

I drove west over the black-tar curving road and pulled up at the junction to Del Mar. "There wasn't anything inside Willie's den. I looked but I didn't know what for. Maybe you can tell me what I'm supposed to have dug up. After that, I'd like to know who you are and what you're doing up here, Hunter."

He nodded, put up the gun. "You first."

"For openers, I'm the guy who got you out of the spa. They had been working on you with drugs to block out your memory. Maybe you don't remember."

He patted the gun in his pocket. "I remember. That's why you're still living."

"Try this one on your memory bank. I muscled George Glendon, the spa director, into springing you free. I got him to help me load you into my car. Before I could say thanks, somebody threw a knife into him."

He shook his head. "Too bad I missed it. I must have conked out."

"I brought you over to a friend of mine. Allie Riegel. Security boss at Del Mar track. I thought you'd be safe there. I forgot to wonder how safe Allie would be."

"Sorry, I didn't know who the hell he was. I had business elsewhere. What brought you to me at the spa anyway?"

I put on the record starting with Willie winning the hundred-grander Princess Stakes at Del Mar and being wiped out the same night. "Allie called me in on it. It's my line and I knew Willie for a lot of years. Allie told me Pam Clayton was missing since Labor Day morning. That gave me two to start with."

"Any luck so far?"

"I keep finding new people with other problems. You're one of them." I filled him in on the other sequences, the red-head up at Tahoe, Glendon and Dorn.

"Who do you figure knocked off Dorn?" he asked.

"You're a pretty good possibility. My friend Allie Riegel is a big strong man. He'd hate to admit you laid him out for more than a ten count. You took off with his car. That gun in your pocket looks like his, right out of the glove compartment. Two slugs like it took a lot of Dorn's head off."

"Nobody will ever miss him," Hunter said laconically. "You still don't know who killed Willie Rich, and you haven't found Pam Clayton."

"I'm way behind," I admitted. "I don't even know who the hell you are."

"My name is Hunter. You seem familiar with Monica Clayton's background. When she was Monica Moore, the famous movie star, she married Jeff Hunter. He was my brother."

"That was twenty years ago. Why are you up here now? It's a long way from Acapulco."

"Willie brought me."

"How did he do that? Did you know each other?"

"Sure. From way back when he knew Jeff. He knew Monica then, too. Maybe you don't know it, but he brought those lovebirds together. Introduced Jeff to Monica, way back then.

"You may know Jeff died pretty soon after they got married. It might have lasted six months. We got the coroner's report. Overdose of barbiturates. Well, we were pretty broken up over it, but what the hell—those things happen and we'd heard a lot about what a tough town Hollywood is. We never figured Jeff to be an actor. But that's what he wanted and we wished him luck.

"A month ago I got a letter from Willie. He said he had found proof Jeff had been murdered. That it wasn't all that accidental. There were two people he named that could be responsible. One was Wesley Dorn. The other was Monica Moore."

I stared at the lanky man beside me. "It doesn't sound like Willie. I haven't seen the official coroner's report myself, but I've been told the details. What kind of proof did Willie say he had? Also, isn't it kind of strange it took so long to turn up? I happen to know a little about Monica Clayton's background, maybe a lot more than you do. She's been a patsy for Louis Charnock and Dorn for years. Dorn has been blackmailing her ever since she started in movies. He hasn't stopped—" I remembered suddenly my visit to Dorn's houseboat. "She's been paying and paying—up till tonight. She's free now. I'd hate to think that alleged letter from Willie was a phony. One more lead to a very unlucky lady."

Hunter shrugged. "I don't know how Willie found the proof. But according to what he told me, it's no fake. He somehow found my brother Jeff's diary. There's supposed to be something in it connecting Monica and Dorn with his death."

"It would have been a pretty neat trick," I said. "You don't get a chance too often to make notes in a diary after people have poisoned you. More generally, you die right away."

"Maybe you do and maybe you don't. When I find the diary, I'll know for sure."

"Is that what I was supposed to have found in Willie's house tonight?"

Hunter nodded. "I know he had it. He never got a chance to show it to me, or tell me where he kept it."

I remembered Pauli, the Claytons' maid, telling me of the attempted phone calls and visits. "Is that why you've been trying to see Tyler Clayton? You don't even have the proof yet and you're trying to put the finger on Monica?"

Hunter ignored the acid in my tone. "It's not the way you think. I knew Clayton married her a year ago. I wasn't too happy about it then and tried to stop it."

I scratched my head. "Maybe you had a good reason."

"I had a different reason then. If Tyler Clayton married the woman who murdered my kid brother, I thought maybe he ought to know about it."

"Sure. Maybe you had a better reason this time."

"Matter of fact, I did. You see, Ty Clayton is my brother."

The little wheels spun around in my head. "You say your name is Hunter. He says his is Clayton."

"We were all Claytons. Ty, myself and little Jeff."

"Where was all this?"

"Born in Melfort, Saskatchewan. Canada. Our mother married Avery Clayton, a lumberman. He died when we were kids. She got a new husband a few years later. John Hunter. Jeff was seven then. I was ten. Ty, the oldest, was twelve.

"Our new dad wanted to adopt us, take his name. But when a kid is twelve, he doesn't have to be adopted if he doesn't want to. Same with changing his name. Ty kept our real dad's. Jeff and I became Hunters. It's that simple."

I remembered Clayton grinning, bragging that he'd been a hunter all his life. I've always hated inside jokes. "If you're brothers, why aren't you welcome at his house? I heard he won't take phone calls from you and refuses to let Pam have anything to do with you."

"That's unfortunate," he said. "We've had a big misunderstanding about some old business."

"That doesn't tell me very much. You don't seem too put out about it. You risked your life to find his daughter at the spa. I understand Willie made the arrangements. Why?"

"I guess he still felt responsible for what happened. I'll tell you why Ty and I been feuding. We had a pact, you see, and he broke it."

"You can tell me about it. I might be dead by morning."

"Well, I never did take much stock in that coroner's report about Jeff. Neither did Ty. We both thought Monica had something to do with it. I was in trouble and had to leave the states, headed back to Mexico. Ty gave me his word he'd stay with it, looking for evidence against Monica. The next thing I knew, after his wife Audrey died, he married her. I read about it in a paper down there.

"At first, I was sore as hell. I wrote him about it. I got a letter from him pretty damn quick, telling me not to worry myself about it, that he hadn't forgotten. I got the idea that he married Monica hoping to find out the truth about her. That was a year ago and he still hasn't done a damn thing and I'm up here now to find out why. If she's guilty according to Jeff's diary, dammit, then Ty will have to do something about it."

"He's not the only one involved here," I said. "Does Monica know Tyler is a Hunter, that she married her first husband's older brother?"

"I don't know. I can't see him telling her if he's out to get her."

"But she was married to Jeff for half a year. He might have told her something about his family. She might have known all along and kept that knowledge to herself."

"Yep," Hunter said. "That's possible."

"Okay, then. I can see your brother Ty wanting to keep

you out of it, if he has a plan going. But what if you're wrong? What if he married Monica only because she happens to be a very pretty, sexy lady?"

"We had a pact," he growled. "Ty wouldn't do that."

"Maybe, maybe not. You'll find out soon enough. Now tell me why you've had the big rush on for Ty's daughter? Pam apparently never even knew she had an Uncle Tom in Mexico."

"She does now. Willie told her." He pounded his fist. "Maybe she started to ask questions, and that's what got her in trouble. Maybe she saw the diary. Pam never cottoned to the idea of Ty hitching up with Monica. No matter how you cut it, she's in Monica's way. The kid's in a dangerous spot."

"How do you figure that?"

"Willie could have told Monica she was in trouble now. For all Monica knew, he'd pass the secret to Ty. Maybe she knocked Willie off to keep him from talking. If she was too late, she'd have to get rid of Ty, to save her own neck."

"And Pam Clayton?"

Hunter shrugged and rubbed his big hands together. "It depends on what the kid knows, and if she's talked. Maybe that's why that guy Glendon got himself killed. The same with her old pal Dorn. He knew too much about her, and he had to go. Anybody who gets in Monica's way has to get it. Figure it out for yourself."

Twenty-four

I settled back in my seat to figure it out and my hand found the .38 I keep there. Hunter never saw it coming and I laid it on him behind the ear. He probably had a good case against Monica, but I like to make up my own mind.

It wasn't far to Allie Riegel's house. He opened the door when I honked and came out. He looked down at Hunter sleeping peacefully at my side. "This is where I came in," he said.

"See if you can hold him this time. I've got things to do."

Allie opened the door and dragged him out. "What happened to him this time?"

"I knocked him out."

"You shouldn't have done that," Allie said. "It was my turn." He sounded genuinely aggrieved. "Where's my car?"

"He was waiting outside Willie Rich's house. I guess you'll find it there."

"What the hell was he doing there?"

"Looking for something."

"Like what?"

"Something Willie had stashed away."

Allie shrugged. "A lot of places Willie could have stashed something."

"I know," I said. "I'm heading for one right now."

. . .

Under a full moon, Del Mar seemed eerily quiet. Horses dozed fitfully on their feet, pawing the ground as they dreamed. The old gray mare nickered in her stall as I shook Joey Zale awake. He didn't waste time collecting his bearings. "He ain't here."

"Who ain't here?"

"Hunter. The dude from Mexico. That's who you're out for, ain't it?"

"It was, but now it ain't because I found him."

"He's a tough cookie," Zale said. "What the hell's he doing up here anyway?"

"Looking for something."

Zale shrugged. "It figures. You mean, besides Clayton's kid?"

I nodded. "Willie didn't leave anything with you for me, Joey, did he? Or did I ask you that before?"

"I don't remember. All I remember is he didn't. Like what?"

I shook my head and tried to picture Willie's last day at Del Mar. After he won the Princess Stakes, he had to weigh in with the stewards, carrying his saddle.

I grinned suddenly, knowing I had it. "What happened to Willie's gear after the weigh-in?"

"He took it back to the jocks' room."

"Is it still there?"

Zale shook his head. "No. I cleared out his gear."

"Where's the saddle, Joey?"

He shifted, looked worried, lit a cigarette. "Aw, c'mon, Roper—have a heart. I can get fifty bucks for it."

I peeled out my billfold. "Here's a hundred. Where is it?"

Zale looked down.

"Don't tell me you've sold it already, Joey!" I yelled.

He shook his head, surprised. "No. It's right here. I been sleeping on it."

He looked at me curiously as I shoved the money at him and grabbed for the saddle. When a jockey's weight is insufficient to meet the impost of his mount, lead is placed in the pockets of his saddle. The lead is dead weight and brings the weight carried up to the mount's impost. Its effect in a reduction of a horse's speed is greater than an equivalent live weight, because unlike a jockey's weight, it cannot be shifted forward to facilitate his efforts to speed the horse.

Zale saw my hands at the pockets. "If it'll help you any, Calamity's assigned weight for the Princess was a hundred and ten. Willie weighed a hundred and twelve. He was packing a two-pound overweight. I think I left the plates upstairs in the jocks' room."

I didn't pay much attention to what Zale was saying. It was deep inside the pocket, red leather-bound with a lock on it. The word "Diary" was embossed in slanted gold letters. I looked for a little key but didn't find any.

I dug in my pocket for a matchbook folder, struck the match. As the flame sputtered there was a loud whinny from the open stall. Angry hooves pounded the floor.

"You better put out that match," Joey warned. "Sister Sally gets nervous. She got trapped in a barn one time in a helluva fire."

I blew out the match. The old mare neighed noisily for me to watch it next time.

It turned out it wasn't necessary. The lock to the diary was broken. I flipped it open. It gave the name and address of Jeff Hunter on the opening page. A little printed card pasted behind the front cover read: TO BE NOTIFIED IN CASE OF ACCIDENT. Under it was handwritten Tom Hunter's name and an address in Acapulco, Mexico.

The diary started on New Year's Day and there were brief handwritten notations for almost half the little book. I remembered his marriage to Monica Moore had lasted approximately six months.

Zale was watching me. "A book, huh? Any good?"

"Not bad."

"What the hell is it—some kind of system?"

"Looks like it—for killing people."

The diary account ended as abruptly as his life. The last

page had been ripped out. If Jeff Hunter had written down his killer's name, the information was no longer there.

"You get a lot of visitors, Joey?"

"You mean lately?"

"Since Labor Day. Make it a little before."

"What the hell—Clayton's always here. He's got Calamity and a lot of other horses. Monica's been here. She's got her mare. The kid's been around. She owns Mary Jane, the filly. But they got a right to be around. I wouldn't call them strictly visitors, would you?"

"It doesn't matter. Who else?"

"Well, Cap Abbott's been here. But he lives here, too, like me. Kilburn's been here."

"When was Kilburn here last?"

"I guess Saturday. Two days before Labor Day."

"Any special reason? I know he was Willie's agent."

"They had some discussion, or maybe you could call it a big argument about something. Something Willie wanted to do that Kilburn didn't go along with."

"Anybody else?"

"That dude from Acapulco—Hunter. He's been around. Allie Riegel drops around, looks the place over a lot. That's his job, ain't it?—security."

"Who else?"

Zale shrugged thin shoulders. "People. I don't get all the names. There was some big blond crew-cut guy around, looked like an ex-pug. I don't know what the hell he wanted here. Cap had a guard run him off."

Jay Jay.

"What about Penny? Does she ever drop over?"

"Sometimes. Not too often. You know, she never let on to Willie, but I think Penny really likes the track. She digs horses. They dig her, too. Always nuzzling up to her."

"How about Johnny Cashio?"

Zale shook his head. "I see him around the track. But never back here. With his connections, they'd run Johnny out like a shot."

I held the little book out in front of Zale. "Willie ever show this to you?"

"Never saw it before. That's why I asked was it a system."

"You didn't know he had it stashed in his bag?"

Zale laughed, showing me a lot of yellow tobacco-stained choppers. "It couldn't be there because the stewards look your saddle over. They're always looking for those little electrical gizmos, you know. All that's supposed to be in those side pockets is your lead weights. Willie must have stashed that away the last minute."

"Were you Willie's groom?"

"Yeah, sometimes."

"Then if he kept the book in his room at jock quarters, you'd have noticed it."

"The only trouble is," Zale said slowly, "I never did. It's only a little book. He coulda kept it in his coat pocket. I only helped him get dressed. I never went through his pockets."

I tossed the saddle back to him. "It's all yours. Pleasant dreams."

Twenty-five

I rested my bones so they would stop complaining and got up late the next day. A lot of my nerves and muscles had a hangover from Glendon's isotron and I humored them and twitched a little. A good breakfast straightened out the raw edges, I drank a pot of coffee, soothed my lungs with some smoke, and I was ready. I got the little sticker I had peeled off Willie's desk. I stared at the lettering and wondered about ghosts of the past. "La Cienega Auction House" was printed on it. The address was in Beverly Hills. Underneath was the lot number. I got them on the phone to find out if they were still in business. They said they were, and I finished dressing and drove down there.

"Sonenberg here," a little bald man said. "What was it you couldn't discuss over the phone? You breaking up maybe and you don't want your wife to know you're selling the furniture?"

I explained I had a different problem and showed him the little sticker. "It goes back twenty years," I said.

"I can tell that," he said. "So what's your problem?"

"If you still have your records, perhaps you can tell me what this sticker was on, who sold it, and the name of the buyer."

"That's all you want?"

"If you have all those answers, I might want to give you this twenty-dollar bill," I told him.

He waved it away. "What's twenty dollars nowadays? Now, if you had some good furniture—"

"As soon as I get married and we break up, I'll get in touch with you."

"Okay. See that you don't forget," he said and turned away. He waved to the furniture piled wall to wall. "If you see something you like meanwhile, don't hesitate to buy. A girl you can always get later."

He was back in ten minutes. He looked at me and shook his head. "You didn't see anything you liked?"

"I've saved it for what you're going to show me about the sticker."

"Okay," he said. "I once made a lot of money on this sale, so I'll be good to you. The sticker was for lot M-CLED 3 and that means, according to my books, the party who sold it was Moore. First name, Monica. Once a very popular movie star. The CLED is the price. We use the code word "Cumberland." The numbers go from one to aught. So the price was seventeen hundred and fifty dollars. The number three tells me it was a desk. The books said it was a period piece, Empire, a big sonofagun. The buyer was a Mr. Willie Rich."

He handed me a scrap of paper with the information written down. "Also it was sixteen years ago, not twenty. As I recall, the husband died, and she sold everything in the house. That doesn't happen too often with women, you know. They take a big loss that way. In my experience, when they do that, it's been a big tragedy and they don't want to live with it or be reminded about it any more."

I told him I could understand that.

"The other times," he went on, "Miss Moore did it different. After the cowboy, she sold her place with the furniture; the same with the hotel man. The last time we auctioned for her was after she broke up with that big bunch of muscles. He wanted half of everything, which I suppose he was entitled to under California community property law, but we had a hell of a time. He kept coming around, saying this was his, not hers, and so on.

"That was about ten years ago, and since then I hope she managed to get somebody and hold on to him. She was a nice woman, in my opinion."

I told him the latest in the marriages of Monica Moore.

The old guy nodded, looking pleased. "Clayton, you say? The oil man? Well, good for her. Money never hurt anybody. That's not only an opinion, I think maybe it's gospel. Now what else can I do for you, young fellow?"

"Maybe you can tell me what makes that desk worth so much money?" I said.

"That's no money for a desk like that," he said. "It's a genuine antique, period piece, and these Napoleonic jobs are hard to get. It's a man's desk usually, maybe because it's so big. Maybe they like it because it has a special secret drawer, in case you don't want the little woman to know where you keep your money stashed. I can get thirty-five hundred for it today easily."

I tried to picture Jeff Hunter writing a secret diary, keeping it locked up in a secret desk drawer. Dying without Monica knowing their lives were being put down on paper. It was possible Willie had triggered the secret drawer recently and made his discovery. Hunter's notes had set him off trying to right an old wrong, and every step he took led inexorably to his own death.

As diaries went, this wasn't a literary event. I hoped Hunter had been a better actor than he was a writer. The entries for the first two months were premarital. He met Monica at the track through Willie and came down with an instant crush. He wrote some poetry about how he felt. It was pretty bad. The kind that sells well to the kids today. They were married in March. His brother Tom came up for the wedding. Ty was someplace in Texas trying to cap a big oil well that had blown sky-high.

They waited till Willie won the last race at Bay Meadows

up in San Mateo to get hitched so Willie could be best man. Monica followed the ponies, too. They were at old Del Mar a lot. It was old even then.

The Hunters had a spat before they got home. The house belonged to Monica, but Jeff had brought in some of his own furnishings. I supposed the desk was his, although he didn't mention it. The bride and groom retired to separate bed-chambers.

His notation for that day also read: *March 13. Hell of a way to start a marriage. Saw that creep Dorn hanging around and told her that was all over, old buddies were out. Mon said she would see who she damn well pleased. I told her I'd break his goddam neck. She laughed.*

The following weeks saw them putting things straight for a few days. It blew up again shortly, another argument, wild fights, heavy drinking on both sides. They would be out of touch for long periods. Monica would simply take off, return after a weekend, refusing to explain. She owed him no accounting, she told him.

Hunter hired a private detective in May to tail Monica and Dorn. He reported she took off with another man, never identified. The private eye was fired.

Hunter was working seldom, dating and screwing around a lot. While he kept writing about this great big crush he had on his wife, he was laying all the broads in town. Encounter-group therapy wasn't an in thing in those days.

They made up, fought some more. It sounded like the typical Hollywood movie-star marriage. Hunter got a part in a movie in July. It meant going to Arizona on location. Monica was busy on her own feature. He found a little starlet in Arizona. The nights weren't so cold. He was back in August for the ponies.

August 11. Del Mar. San Clemente Stakes. 3-year-olds, fillies. Willie won four straight. Home with $2,500. Good day!

August 20. Del Mar. Sorrento Stakes. 2-year-olds, fillies. Willie hot again. 3 out of 5. Great party later at Kilburn's beach house. Mon cut out with Dorn. Screw them. Found cute blonde—Sharon something. Lives Laurel Canyon. 2 roomies. Cutting Willie in. Got loaded. Woke up next day with Sharon. Willie next bed over with the two roomies. He can get away with it. He's not married.

August 27. Del Mar. De Anza Stakes. Willie rode 5, lost them all. Blew 2 G's. Tried to borrow money from Mon. Saw her get it from Dorn. Cut out with cute blonde. Elsie Farmer. Asked her if she was the farmer's daughter. She said why didn't I come over sometime and find out. Tried it and not bad. Home dawn. Mon not there. Some jerk on the phone asking for her.

August 31. Stomach hurting lately. Burning. Can't keep food down. Doc out of town. Same jerk still calling. Wants to buy time with Mon. Told him to eat his heart out.

Hunter was back at Del Mar on September 4. It was the Escondido Handicap, for three-year-olds and up. Willie rode four races, lost all but one, a one-to-five favorite. Hunter blew two G's. He summed up his entry later: *Waiting for Mon. 12 P.M. Terrible stomach pains again. Got to have this out with her. Took some of her pills. Pains worse. 2 P.M. Vomited . . . burning stomach pains . . . I wonder who they're trying to kill here . . . think I know why . . . phone ringing . . . all night . . .*

If he found out, he never told me. The next page was ripped out of the binding. On September 6, Hunter was dead.

The clerk at the coroner's office took my two dollars and dug up a certificate of death, stamped: THIS IS A TRUE CERTIFIED COPY OF THE RECORD FILED IN THE LOS ANGELES COUNTY HEALTH DEPARTMENT IF IT BEARS THE SEAL IMPRINTED IN PURPLE INK.

It looked purple to me.

A completed autopsy and preliminary toxicological examination revealed the "cause of death appeared to be that of an overdose of drugs . . . one of which has been identified as a barbiturate."

Alcohol content in blood rates .09 for two highballs.

They gave Hunter a better mark. Alcohol in the blood mg per cc: 3.0.

The three-point-ohers are breathing heavily, in a stuporous condition. They have no comprehension of language. They will strike wildly at any person who tries to help them.

Pill-popping and washing it down with booze is a real downer. Nobody has to kill you, because you're doing it all to yourself. A depression of the nervous system follows, leading to coma and fatal results telling you too late you can't combine alcohol with phenobarbital. It can take as little as an hour. With the tranquilizers, the phenothiazines, it can be just as quick. Death from asphyxia due to aspiration.

Box thirty-three of the page was marked: "Specify accident, suicide or homicide." Handwritten was the word "accidental."

"How do they know when it's accidental?" I asked the clerk.

"They don't," she said. "Sometimes it's suicide. How do you know what was in the victim's mind?" She smiled, put her finger on a line near the top, the box for listing the name of surviving spouse (if wife, enter maiden name). "Surviving spouse makes a statement which is taken as evidence. It stands unless there is conflicting evidence to the contrary, or such as to make it extremely doubtful and insupportable. 'Suicide' is a bastard to put down, anyway. It raises hell with collecting insurance policies. 'Accidental' makes it easier for everybody in the family. Also, there's no stigma."

The box in the lower right-hand corner was for the signature of the physician or coroner. It was signed "Paul Stokes, M.D."

The date of Hunter's death was typed "September 6." In a small box adjacent was written the time: "Prior to 10 A.M."

His age was thirty-six years.

The place of death was given, the address in Brentwood. Burial was specified. Holly Memorial Park. It gave the name of the funeral director and his place of business. Los Angeles.

Hunter's death certificate answered other questions. He was born in Melfort, Saskatchewan, Canada. He had become a citizen of the United States. Under name and birthplace of father it read: John Hunter—unknown. Maiden name and birthplace of mother: Helen Young—Broken Drum, Saskatchewan, Canada.

Monica Moore was listed as his surviving spouse. His given occupation was actor.

I asked the clerk where I could get in touch with Dr. Stokes.

"No way," she said. "He's dead."

"When did he die?"

"About fifteen years ago. Like that."

"Did you know him?"

She shook her head. "The reason I know is somebody looked it up for a party who was interested."

"What killed him?"

"Car accident. Hit-and-run."

I showed her the death certificate. "About this date?"

She nodded. "That's right. Maybe a week later."

"Do you remember who was asking about Dr. Stokes?"

She shook her head again. "I didn't catch his name. He was a little fellow, though. I remember that."

"When was this?"

"Not too long ago. Maybe a month. That's how come I can remember."

I called my pal at Homicide, Camino. He asked where I was. I told him and he grunted. "Okay. Come on over. I got a sore tooth anyway. I won't be able to blame that on you."

He was rubbing his jaw when I came through the door.

"Rubbing won't make that kind of swelling go away," I told him. "It's probably an impacted wisdom tooth."

Camino's eyes rolled. "If I had any wisdom teeth left, I wouldn't be talking to you. Let's hear what you've got."

I told him and he listened.

"Sounds fantastic," he said finally. "More improbable maybe than even an impacted wisdom tooth."

I showed him the diary and he looked through it, dropped it finally, and shot me a questioning look. "You don't have the last page of it?"

"Not yet, Nick." I handed him the copy of Hunter's death certificate. "He was buried at Holly Memorial Park. Stokes was killed immediately afterward. Maybe it wasn't an accident."

Camino tapped the paper. "I could have the body dug up. Exhuming Hunter would require a court order and I could probably get it. It would be better if you got permission from his immediate family."

"I know. But I might have somebody else murdered then."

He nodded, his face twisted with pain. "Christ! What are you expecting to find—arsenic? That went out of style a long time ago."

"Maybe the killer didn't know it at the time."

Camino stared glumly. "Let's suppose we found something. You know as well as I do, that where arsenic's concerned, it leaves traces—if the organs are gone, it'll be in the bones, or the hair, the fingers or toenails. But you still have to prove your suspect had possession, administered it, and be able to state where and when. Can you do that?"

I knew as well as he did I couldn't.

He picked up the diary, rubbing his hurting jaw savagely. "If that isn't enough, you can't produce this diary as evidence, either. Hunter died and can't confirm it. It doesn't clinch anything so far as I'm concerned."

"That's okay," I said. "It could be a fake anyway. Maybe Hunter never wrote it."

Camino scowled. "Great," he said. "That makes another thing you can't prove." He picked up his phone. "Speaking about things you know for sure, what's that thing I've got wrong with my jaw?"

"Impacted wisdom tooth. I had the same symptoms once and—"

He was dialing before I could finish. "Hi, Doc," he said cheerfully into the phone, "a friend just told me I've an impacted wisdom tooth and—" He broke off, listened. "The hell you say! Thanks, Doc." He hung up, nodding to me with curled lip. "That was my dentist. He said I don't have any more wisdom teeth. He took out the last of them two years ago."

I shook my head. "It sure fooled me."

I went over it all again in my mind. Whether the diary was genuine or not, everything appeared to hinge upon Willie's discovery of it. I knew only a small part of the waves he had made. Only the killer would know how big they really were, how totally engulfing they might be.

I thought about everybody connected with Willie Rich who might have a particular reason for wanting him dead. I thought about the missing diary page. I thought about the missing Miss Clayton and why it was so damn difficult to find her.

I thought it was about time I went for the killer.

Twenty-six

They were running the Del Mar Futurity. It was for two-year-olds, seven and a half furlongs on turf, a big $60,000 event. I called Tyler Clayton to find out if he was running Calamity.

"I'm sorry, nobody is home," the singsong voice said.

"Pauli? This is Roper. Are they at the races?"

"Yes. Miss Pam is not home yet."

"I still expect to find her. Do you remember we were talking about Labor Day? There was a big party, you said, at the house."

"Yes. Your friend, Mister Willie, he was not there. I have tried to think about it. No, he was not."

"All right. Were Mr. and Mrs. Clayton there all evening?"

"What a question! Of course, Mr. Detective. It was their party, no?"

"I mean, did either of them leave the party at all at any time. Later in the evening. For perhaps an hour."

"Oh, yes, Mr. Clayton left. But he had to."

"Why?"

"We were out of his—his drinks. He needed to buy some Scotch, he said."

"Did he usually do his own shopping?"

"No. But it was a very big party."

"It was Labor Day evening. A holiday. Weren't the stores closed?"

"Yes, you are right. He told me so after."

"He came back without the booze?"

"No. He had it—the booze. Four bottles, he had."

"Did he say where he got it?"

"A friend, he said. He said he was lucky he had some rich friends. He was laughing about it."

"I'd be laughing, too. What about Mrs. Clayton? Was she at home all evening?"

"Well, of course. But she, too, had to go out for some little while, not for long. A friend had to leave early. Her car would not start. So Mrs. Monica took her home then."

"What time was this?"

"Nearly ten o'clock."

"Do you know the friend's name and where she lived?"

"It was Mrs. Jackson. She lives in Escondido, near to your friend."

"Willie Rich?"

"Yes. They are neighbors. Her husband died. He was a friend of Mr. Clayton a long time, also in the horses business."

"Do you know when Mr. Jackson died?"

"Perhaps a year ago. Do you always ask only questions?"

"That's how you make a living if you don't know the answers."

"Don't forget I am a Swedish girl. Are you going to kiss me again?"

"I'd kiss you right now if I had the time."

"You are still looking for your killer?"

"I think right now we're looking for each other."

Calamity was fussing around in the gate when the break came. She was stuck on the inside and seemed out of it. Pierce was riding and managed to get her out at the quarter pole. She caught the pacemaker, Determined, in the middle of the far turn, then drew away once straightened out in the stretch to win by a length and a half. Calamity's time was 1:31 and she paid $4.20.

I watched Tyler Clayton go down to join Pierce in the winner's circle. Monica Clayton looked startled but lovely when I touched her elbow. There was nobody else in their box.

"I have to know something now," I said, "and I'd rather hear it from you."

She smiled. "That sounds like a familiar scene, Mr. Roper." She turned her head to look down at her husband below. "Are you picking this moment because Tyler is down there?"

"Yes. It's about your first husband."

"You're referring to Jeff Hunter? It wouldn't do to get them mixed up, in the wrong order."

"Jeff Hunter. I saw the death certificate today. It was marked accidental death. Did you agree with that?"

"How could I?" she said. "I was certain he was murdered—just as you are."

"But you weren't responsible—any more than you were for Willie's drowning?"

The beautiful eyes flashed. "I didn't kill either of them. 'Responsible' is another word completely. I've accepted that."

"I'm ready to make my move," I said. "One name from you would make it a lot easier."

She tossed the flaming strawberry set carelessly. "I'm sure it would. Perhaps too easy. If you know anything at all, then you'll know I can't possibly help you."

I shrugged. "If that's your final word—"

Her lips framed a friendly smile. "Did you win on Calamity?"

"Yes. I had—"

The smile turned chilly. "*Well,* then," she said. "There's your answer."

190

I nodded. "That's cute, but not good enough. Did you know Jeff Hunter left a diary behind when he died? That it's turned up recently?"

She reacted, went into the familar pose. Curved hand to throat. Parted lips. Rapidly rising breasts. A good, good show. She ran it for all it was worth, then shook her head. "No," she said hoarsely. "I didn't."

"Too bad," I said. "He knew somebody was killing him, too."

I left her staring helplessly, a lovely hunk of woman it was murder to get too close to. My hands were wet and clammy. With all I knew, she could still turn me on.

Charnock answered his phone on the third ring.

"Your situation is different now," I told him. "I hope you're able to resume a normal life again soon."

His voice was firmly resonant, under control. "I still haven't adjusted to it, Mr. Roper. Dorn has been part of me for so long, I'm not certain I can function without him."

"You can do it. It's all in your books."

He laughed. "Thank you. I must remember to read one of them tonight."

"Things on my end are nearly resolved, too," I said. "I have a problem with one of the parties concerned, though, and I'd appreciate any help you could give me."

"Monica?"

"Yes. She's in this more than she realizes. If I could have a few moments with you, perhaps we could find some way to make her actions less accountable."

He asked where I was and I told him. "There's still time before I leave for my lecture in San Diego. Why don't you drop by for a few minutes? I'm sure it's Dorn they wanted, not her, anyway. Perhaps I do know enough to clear her. Now that I've a chance again, I'd like to afford her the same, if I can. No matter what you believe, Mr. Roper, I contend Monica has always been an innocent. A victim—as I was."

"I'll be right over." . . .

It was dusk when I pulled up to the cottage at the far end fronting the bay. I could see Dorn's houseboat dimly through the haze. I didn't see Charnock's big black car or the blond bodyguard, Jay Jay, anywhere on the lot.

"Come in, Mr. Roper. You look tired."

"It's been a rough week. Did you mean what you said about helping Monica Clayton?"

"Certainly." He ushered me inside to a soft chair. The room was well lit, well furnished. This was the living room. A door to the kitchenette was open, another to the bedroom closed. Several of Charnock's books were scattered around the sofa and tables, and yellow pads covered with scribbled heavy lines. He started to tidy up, stacking the notes and books separately.

"Writing another book?"

He smiled gently. "Hardly. At least not yet. I'll wait until my mind clears. No, these are notes for this evening's lecture. It's so easy to repeat oneself, and I do like to make new and fresh impressions on people. I haven't for some time now. Perhaps it's because of what's happened—this sudden release—"

"Maybe I'll have the same good feeling after tonight."

"Tonight? Are you really that close?"

I nodded. "It wasn't that difficult, really. I've just been making it more than it was. It's been right there under my nose all the time."

He adjusted the lamp, sat opposite me leaning back comfortably, twining his long white hands. "I've no expertise in your field, and I'd hate to contradict you. But I might as well warn you that I feel it hardly likely that Monica could be the person you're looking for. True, she suffered for many years under Dorn's domination, just like me, but—" He shook his head slowly several times. "I know her too well, you see. She's simply not the type to be a murderer."

I smiled. "Then you don't know too much about murder or women, Charnock. For one thing, there's no such thing as type. Anybody can be a killer, given the reason. For another, women, bless their neat tidy secretive hearts, can be among the best when it comes to murder."

"I'm sorry," he said coldly, "I can't agree. Admittedly it's your profession, and you've become casehardened. I see people differently. It's the rare one, in my experience, who will sin. But I'll be quiet and hear your evidence." He cleared his throat nervously. "Hopefully, I can prove you're wrong."

"I hope you can. That's why I'm here. I like Mrs. Clayton. I feel sorry for anybody who's been a sucker for a long time. But let's get one thing straight. I'm not saying she's the killer I'm after."

He looked pleased and surprised. "But I thought—"

I shook the old head. "Responsible, maybe—maybe positively, even. But not the killer. This all goes back about sixteen years, you see. Starting with the death of her first husband, Jeff Hunter."

Charnock stiffened. "Surely you're not suggesting she—"

"I'm not suggesting anything yet. I'm just starting it in order. You were close to her at that time. You might remember something about it. They were only married a short time. Less than a year. Hunter died one night from an overdose of sleeping pills."

Charnock frowned. "That could have been accidental, you know. There are tensions in a new marriage, as indeed there are in any. I would agree that both parties as a rule are responsible to each other mutually, but I've heard of many such instances. Unfortunate though they may be, there are many reasons—"

"Did you ever meet Hunter?"

"Well, yes—I believe I did. Once or twice. At parties, perhaps we said hello."

"Did he seem a suicidal type?"

Charnock shook his head vehemently. "I'm sorry, but who is to say? Can you really classify people that casually?"

"Sometimes you can. What about your friend Dorn? Can you see him messing up their affair somehow?"

"Dorn?" Charnock's sensitive face clouded and his lips set grimly. "I see what you mean. You're referring now to the information I gave you—the hold he had on Monica, the prints of her unfortunate film."

"You'll agree Dorn wasn't the type to let go. He'd go after whatever he could to get the most out of his situation, wouldn't he? What if he was playing both ends?"

"I don't understand," Charnock murmured helplessly.

"You told me he was collecting from Monica, blackmailing her with what he had on her. Wasn't Dorn the type to use what he had on her husband, too? Squeeze what he could out of him the same way, to suppress something that would have ruined her career? He had even more to work with this time —their marriage."

Charnock sank his head in his hands and was silent for a few moments. When he looked up, his eyes were filmy, haunted. "It's my fault," he said brokenly. "If I had been more of a man—stood up to him—it was only because of my weakness Dorn could continue to exist—and prosper."

"Don't blame yourself. It wouldn't have been that easy. He had you over a barrel, too."

He shook his head, his mouth a bitter grieving line. "I'm sorry I can't accept that. There were many ways—I should have found them. What you fear, you know, seldom compares to the reality. We erect our own nightmares to haunt us."

"Sure we do," I agreed. "But let's let that one go for the time being. I thought maybe you might have known something for certain about that period. Something I could pin definitely on who was responsible. I thought Monica was. But it's possible Dorn had her hands tied and could make his moves without her knowledge. Let's skip a lot of time and whatever went on with them and bring it up to the present, where I came in. Because if she was innocently involved then, she's up to her neck in it now."

Charnock glanced at his slim gold watch. "Your friend, the jockey?"

"That's where I came in. Willie Rich was killed Monday night. Clayton's daughter has been missing since noon of that day." I ticked them off on my fingers. "A little redhead who worked at the spa where Pam Clayton was headed was murdered up at Lake Tahoe two nights ago. George Glendon, who was the spa director, was killed last night. A little later in the evening, so was your friend Dorn, too.

"That's one drowning. One missing person. Two knife jobs. One shot through the head.

"In addition, another man was kidnapped, held for a while at the spa, beaten up, and drugged to block out his memory. I've been beaten up considerably myself since I got involved. It's been a long tough week chasing after a very busy and clever killer."

Charnock looked shocked. "I admit this all sounds harrowing. But surely Monica couldn't be a part of this—it's preposterous!"

I held my hand up to still the overtones from his ringing voice. "Not Monica. Somebody close to her. Her husband—Tyler Clayton."

Charnock stared again. "Clayton? The millionaire oilman?" His lips twisted wryly and he almost tittered. "My dear Mr. Roper, perhaps you have had too tiring a week—"

I shook the old head stubbornly. "It was Clayton, all right. He did all the tricks. If you care to listen, I'll prove it."

He checked his timepiece again, settled back, folded his hands. "Go ahead. I'm listening. My lecture starts at eight-thirty. That should give you time enough."

The curtains were drawn. Charnock relaxed seemed to convey an aura of peace. A car started occasionally in the parking lot outside, doors slammed, footsteps tramped on the concrete walk, voices filtered into the distance. Charnock's eyes were hooded. I hoped he wasn't asleep.

"It was all triggered a month or so ago. Willie Rich put everything into motion. But again it was all linked with the past.

"After Jeff Hunter died, Monica sold the house, auctioned off her furniture. Willie bought Jeff's desk, an antique, French Empire period. I don't know if he bought it as a favor to Monica to help her out or because he liked it. It's a big desk, a good one for a library. It had something else, a trick secret drawer, built in cleverly behind the front one, which is shallow. I'm assuming Willie only discovered the secret drawer recently. Otherwise all of this might have taken place years ago or been resolved differently.

"In the secret drawer, he found an old diary. Hunter's diary. Willie read it, discovered certain things. He got off a letter to Hunter's older brother Tom in Acapulco, to the effect he had information Hunter had not died accidentally as supposed, but had been murdered. He implied Monica was tied in somehow with the murder plot. He felt responsible because he had brought Jeff and Monica together originally."

"We are all responsible," Charnock droned sonorously. "We are all linked together. It is the law of the cosmos."

"I'm beginning to believe it," I said. "What happened afterward proves your point. Tom Hunter immediately wrote Clayton from Mexico demanding he investigate the matter. You may not be aware, Mr. Charnock, Tyler Clayton is part of the Hunter clan, the oldest brother."

Charnock's eyes flicked open. "Brother?"

I explained the circumstances. "Apparently Clayton took no action and Tom Hunter came up here, a big tough bad-tempered man determined on vengeance. His brother Tyler refused to see him or talk to him. Hunter tried to contact Tyler's daughter and Clayton managed to forbid that.

"Willie didn't go along with Clayton's forget-it attitude. He arranged for Tom Hunter to meet with Pamela, Clayton's kid. In the meantime, he kept the pressure on, and he must have informed Clayton finally about what he had. You've got to remember that Willie knew Monica from the past and he recalled your old friend Dorn being around her."

Charnock's eyes glittered. "Ah, yes. Dorn again."

"Labor Day must have been the deadline Willie allowed

for Clayton to take action. He rode Clayton's horse Calamity for a win in the Princess Stakes, but it was his last race for Clayton. He had already made this clear to his agent Kilburn. It was his last race, period. He was drowned in his own pool that night. Tyler Clayton is big and strong enough to have put Willie down and held him under one-handed."

"I've read a little of accidental drownings," Charnock said gravely. "Your accusation might be difficult to maintain without proof."

"Part of it is conjecture," I admitted, "but wait till you see how it all goes together. Willie's house was broken into, nothing taken. I'm assuming it was Clayton looking for the alleged diary. He never found it. Penny Rich reported another attempt after Willie's death.

"Monday morning Pamela Clayton had an appointment with her hairdresser at the Gilded Cuckoo, a health spa in Poway. Monica Clayton has been a frequent visitor there in the past, for her own personal reasons, drugs, alcoholism, or what have you. The spa was run by George Glendon. My guess is Glendon respected Clayton's pull and power and acted as his flunky, either from fear or because Clayton might have made it worth his while financially.

"Pam Clayton showed up for her morning appointment and was instantly drugged and held prisoner. Glendon admitted this to me. Clayton knew Willie saw a lot of his daughter. He already had made his plans for the evening regarding Willie, and wanted his daughter out of the way. Glendon managed to hold her and changed the books to make it appear she never had an appointment that day.

"Willie knew. He had arranged for her to meet Tom Hunter at Del Mar track. He left word with a stable hand to relay the message to Hunter. When Hunter got to the spa and they told him she had no appointment, he blew his stack and went wild."

"Wildness," Charnock murmured reflectively, "an attribute possessed by the brave. I've often wondered about this demonic gift. A sane person can only marvel at the berserk. Yet, if it could be more reasonably apportioned—we might all rise to challenge our providence."

I blinked and had to remember Charnock would always be bemoaning his cowardice. I continued with what Glendon had told me.

"Memory block? Regression? Whatever for?" Charnock asked.

"Clayton had to make sure his brother would never link his daughter's disappearance with Willie's planned assassination. His plans at this point for his daughter and brother were merely temporary stopgaps. He needed time and freedom for his moves. After he had taken care of Willie, he ordered his daughter's release the following day. His brother was resisting the drug treatment. They had to hold him until they were sure."

Charnock held up a protesting hand. "Surely Monica must have suspected something."

"She suspected plenty. If you recall, she visited you up in L.A. the next night. She wanted to see Dorn, you told me, to pay him money. You were wrong about that, Charnock. She went because she thought Dorn was involved. She thought he was responding to Willie's threat of exposure by snatching Clayton's daughter to use as a bargaining weapon in case things got to be more than he could handle. Perhaps he was beginning to lean on her now too for hush money from Clayton. He had the horn of plenty to draw from since she married him."

Charnock thought about it. "Perhaps you're right. She was very quiet and subdued, almost hostile, when she sat with me in my car that evening. More agitated, too, than I can ever remember."

"Naturally. As far as she was concerned, Dorn was about to cook her new golden goose. Perhaps she warned him he was going too far this time. I think with all she had taken already from Dorn, she still didn't want Clayton's daughter involved. I think she knew, too, that Clayton was a

198

dangerous man to fool around with. Everything might blow up in their faces. I'm even willing to credit Monica with objecting if only on moral grounds. Do what you will to me but leave the girl out of it. Something like that."

"Yes, I'm inclined to agree with you there."

"Dorn, if he knew nothing before, was put on to something different now. He knew he wasn't the cause of Willie's death or Pamela's disappearance. I think he was smart enough to figure out Clayton's angle and his moves. Then he started to work out his own angles. He could have known Glendon too and managed to get a little information about what was going on. I saw him there, later, when they had me caught, and from the treatment I got and the questions put to me, Dorn was very much a part of the picture. When I managed to put things my way, Glendon admitted Dorn was responsible for everything. But then, I think he knew he had more to fear from Clayton and had to protect his identity at any cost."

"A mistake in judgment," Charnock demurred. "My opinion, of course. Go on with your story."

I thought about it, and shook my head. "Perhaps. But taking Tyler Clayton's problem first, after ordering his daughter held, temporarily put out with a mild sedative, then his brother, he had one more loose end. The receptionist on duty had seen Pam Clayton come into the spa for her scheduled appointment. She knew her from previous appointments. Shortly afterward, Hunter barged in, refused to believe Pam wasn't there, broke through to the inside demanding to see his niece. At this stage, Clayton still didn't know which way he was going to move. If his plan misfired, he had another witness—the receptionist.

"Her name was Bonnie Burns. Clayton ordered Glendon to give her her vacation at once, starting that afternoon. She went off to Lake Tahoe. He followed her there and silenced her. Hunting knife in the back."

Charnock shivered. "Incredible," he murmured. "An innocent girl."

I shrugged. "He had to do it. As it turned out, it was the right move for him. I came to the spa yesterday, got my way out of trouble, and twisted Glendon's arm a little. I found Hunter, drugged somewhat and in poor shape, but still sound mentally despite treatment, still insistent upon finding his niece. Glendon assured him she had been released. He helped me put Hunter into my car. I was about to ask him another question when a car pulled in the next lot and somebody threw a knife in him. The killer got away in the dark."

"You're saying that was Clayton again?"

I nodded. "Later that evening, he did you a favor. He got on Dorn's houseboat and put two bullets into his head. I've witnessed the kind of shooting Clayton is capable of. He put two bullets into Dorn's head not an inch apart. I've seen him at his private shooting range do even better at twice the distance."

"Why would he kill Dorn? Apart from seeing his brother at the spa, as you've told me, apparently he was no witness to any particular crime."

"You're right. But then, remember Monica visited Dorn. It's possible he started to try wheeling and dealing with Clayton. Using his blackmail tactics. We know he was at the spa cutting in with Glendon. Clayton was too tough for that. Besides, he already knew from Willie that Dorn was the man who had been blackmailing his wife."

Charnock sat up straighter. "How would you know that?"

I shrugged. "It's partly an assumption. Willie would have had to tell him something. He'd already written Hunter, told him more. He might have told Clayton something of what Hunter wrote in his dairy before he died."

"I'd forgotten that. So then, to finish everything off perfectly, Clayton found the diary, and so far as he could, has protected Monica." He shuddered. "At what cost! What did it gain him in the long run? He'll still have to pay the price for his crimes."

"Maybe not," I said. "For one thing, he still hasn't found the diary."

Charnock smiled, snapping his fingers sharply. "His brother would have it, then. Perhaps your friend Rich gave it to him for safekeeping."

"I doubt that. The last time Willie saw Hunter, he was very much alive. He never dreamed he would be dead that night. If he did, he would have sent me the diary."

"Either you or Clayton's daughter," Charnock said. "You haven't found her yet, you say. He might have left it with her."

I shook my head. "He didn't. He left it in a special place for me to find."

"I see," Charnock said slowly, rubbing his temple as if puzzled. "Apparently it's all over then. You bring Clayton over to the police for the killings and—" He frowned. "You wanted to speak to me concerning Monica. A question of responsibility, wasn't it? Well, she is concerned in the matter, of course, but only as a pawn, an innocent victim. I can't see her being charged with anything. She was nobody's accomplice."

"You're forgetting the original murder," I said. "Her first husband. Jeff Hunter."

Charnock's eyes blazed. "You have no proof, sir. These are all suppositions on your part."

I shook the old noggin again. "Whoever killed Willie Rich killed them all. It goes back from Willie to Jeff Hunter."

Charnock laughed softly. "I'm sorry," he said. "I'm not too good at this sort of thing. Perhaps you've confused me. I don't believe Tyler Clayton ever met Dorn before. Certainly he had no reason to kill his youngest brother."

"That's true," I said. "No matter how often I go over it, that's the one weak link I can't fit."

"Sometimes we force our own errors," Charnock said gravely, "putting stress and emphasis instead of merely turning away. Merely because you have found reasons to suspect Mr. Clayton of so many killings, it doesn't necessarily mean he committed all of them."

"You've a point," I said. "But I'd be willing to bet my life one man did them all."

"It's a wishful thought, Mr. Roper. None of us likes to leave a loose end. You're trying to wrap it all up as one complete package. Logically, you must admit Tyler Clayton could not have killed his own brother."

"That's right," I said. "He couldn't have for the most logical reason of all. *You* did."

He appeared not to have heard. Then he smiled. "My dear man, did I hear you correctly?"

"You killed them all, starting with Hunter. You had me believing your story about Dorn dominating you, blackmailing you into submission all these years. I was right all along. You pulled the strings. You gave the orders. You set up the targets and Dorn had to follow through or you'd mess him up. You killed Dorn along with the rest and, especially, you killed Willie Rich."

He inhaled deeply, and let it out by the numbers. He didn't turn a hair or let his voice off register by a sharp or flat. "That would be difficult to prove, too, with Dorn dead."

"It's part of the proof, Charnock. The killer knocked off everybody who could have had anything on him. The fact that Dorn's dead and you're not cements it. You've only let Monica live because you never thought you'd be caught up. As long as she's married to Tyler Clayton, you know that with what you have on her, your pockets will be lined forever."

"You're wrong, oh, so wrong," Charnock said. "What would it take to convince you?"

"Some luggage, for one thing."

His thick eyebrows flew up. "Luggage?"

"On the way back from Tahoe. You'd spent a week up there, remember?"

He rubbed his head. "What are you talking about? I never spent a week in Tahoe."

"I know you didn't. But you told me you had. We met on the plane coming back. You had just finished killing Bonnie Burns. I'd just found her body. There were only seven passengers aboard. You were a dental surgeon coming down with cancer. You told me you had spent the week up there for a last good look at the blue, blue waters of good old Lake Tahoe."

"A dental surgeon dying of cancer?" he repeated hollowly.

"You had me convinced, too," I said. "All the way back. You've been an actor, you know all the make-up tricks. The best disguise is always the simplest, and you know that, too. A little more eye shadow, hollows for the cheek, always easier when one wears and can remove partial dentures such as you wear. Your performance was flawless until we got off the plane.

"Even a man coming back home to die carries his clothing back with him. You'd spent a week up at Tahoe, you said. That requires change of clothing. It's pretty cold up there. But when we got off the plane, you never wasted a minute going for the baggage room. You headed right for a taxi.

"Coming up there to do a job fast, you didn't need luggage. You did it fast and got right out. The story you improvised just didn't check out, you see. Tough."

His voice dropped a notch, turned rasping and ugly. "It's an utterly ridiculous hypothesis. I suggest you were better off dealing with your original killer, Clayton."

"No, Charnock, you're wrong again. Clayton was my hypothesis. I wondered how far a man like him would go for somebody he really loved. I think Clayton would have done exactly what you did, to protect Monica. Luckily for him, you saved him the trouble. Glendon was your link and pigeon, not his. Like Dorn was. You've been conning and blackmailing people all your life with a respectable front and one of the greatest acts going. It will be a pleasure to put you away."

I didn't see the gun in his hand until too late.

"I doubt you will have the pleasure." He waved the gun briskly. "Get up, please."

"Killing me won't solve your problem, Charnock. I may be the only living witness. But you're forgetting what Jeff Hunter wrote in his diary. There's enough there to burn you."

"You have it?"

I tried shaking my head. He raised the gun to center on my groin. No man with my love of life ever likes to get it there. While I was trying to think of anybody who did, he took a step closer. "Jay Jay," he said softly.

The door behind me opened, and I could smell the big blond bouncer as he walked over softly.

"Where's the diary?" Charnock asked. "Your last chance."

"It's at the track," I said. "Willie hid it good and I'm the only one who—"

Charnock smiled and then something no heavier than a cannon dropped on my head, making him smile even more. As I folded to hit the carpet I noticed my empty hands, lax and useless.

All that karate you know is great stuff, I told myself, and then went rolling down a long black tunnel, bumping along the sides and getting hurt every foot of the way.

Twenty-seven

Cold steel tapped me on the nose. I came up out of the dark tunnel sucking for air. It was only blood blocking my nasal passages. I hurt all over and my head felt too big for the skin around it. They must have been working me over pretty good after I fell. Maybe I got up a few times and the big burly man put me down again. I was too woozy to remember.

"On your feet, and walk slow. Open your mouth and you're dead."

I got on my feet, walked slow. I couldn't walk any better anyway and my lips told me they were too swollen and they didn't want me to talk.

They held me braced between them. The night was dark, with a cool biting wind. The moon floated in the sky, a big lemon balloon without a string on it. I smelled fresh hay and fertilizer. I saw the long string of stalls and heard hooves strike the dirt. A nag nickered somewhere to tell them I was coming.

I've left Del Mar a loser many times. It felt a shame to be coming back that way.

If Allie Riegel had any security men checking his joint, you never would have known it. Jay Jay and Charnock moved in and out, up slopes and down, avoiding the lighted stables where men were working. They seemed to know the place by heart.

"Hold it, Jay Jay."

The big guy didn't have to be told twice by his master. He stopped and hauled me back with him. I leaned against a shed, trying to remember when I had ever felt so tired.

Charnock's eyes were black diamonds glittering in the night. "I'll tell you something, sucker. You were right all along. Nobody knew it, but you guessed it right. I can tell you now how I did it because you'll be dead soon enough.

"Sure, I killed Jeff Hunter. But I did it with imagination. It took only a little of mine and a lot of his. They can dig him up, but they won't find any trace of poison in him. No secret little holes anyplace either.

"I did it mentally. I'm a mentalist, you know. What better way is there for murder? I had nothing against him. It was all Monica's fault, you see. I offered her my love, but she spurned it. She loved Hunter. Well, then, what I was to do? Accept their love as some manifestation from the heavens?

"I had her pictures, the ones she had foolishly made. She thought she had bought back the prints many times. But then, what are prints for if not to be duplicated? I called Hunter. At all times. I told him what I had seen. I offered him money for various pictures of her anatomy. I specified my needs."

"Sounds like good-fun phone conversation," I said thickly, the only way I could talk. "What stopped him from killing you?"

"Why, the prints, the evidence, of course. He knew I had contacts with a lot of shady people, the kind who wouldn't hesitate a second spreading the stuff around the moment he touched me. He knew killing me would only destroy her."

Charnock's laugh couldn't have been any different from the serpent's after Eve borrowed the big apple. "He realized he had no choice. The only way he could stop me was by stopping up his own ears. He chose to take an overdose of Monica's sleeping tablets. He didn't know, of course, that

206

she had collected those pills for her own intended suicide. She thought she had had all of my kind of torture, too. After seeing Jeff Hunter dead in her living room, she lost whatever will she had. You might say she admitted she had lost.

"So, you see, I did kill Hunter. Perhaps not in the way you would have liked, but it was good enough for me. Well, what do you think?"

"It's like I said before. I think you killed him."

"Good boy. Now keep walking until you find the stall or stable where you figure Hunter's diary is. I'm pretty sure you'll be dead after you give it to us. I can't think of a single reason to let you out of it alive. But if you balk, or try a fast one, Monica gets it, too. I'd be willing to wipe it all out now. It's all over and frankly it's been a long bloody bore."

Monica had always been there, decoy, bait, handy door prize men would die for as they had done for all the Monicas in history.

Charnock chuckled. "You were way off on the Tahoe flight. I wasn't the dental surgeon. I was the nutty lady up front with the knitting needles, cutting up the magazines. Pretty good, eh?"

"I know. I checked. He came back later for his bag. He had an errand in L.A. He still had to go on to San Diego. The blond wig left in Bonnie Burns' cabin was a puzzler at first. Later the main lodge keeper remembered a blond woman asking for her. An aunt. The pictures you cut out on the plane typed you as homicidal. The normal ones don't cut off heads." I tried to keep talking, needing time. "You bought two one-way tickets, going up as a blonde, returning dark, wearing a scarf, talking to yourself like a nut to keep people away from you. You left your wool and knitting needles in the john. They'll show your fingerprints."

"I doubt it," Charnock said smoothly. "I wore gloves. Shall we proceed to the diary now?"

The upslope was familiar. I indicated a dark stall. "It's in there." A horse moved restlessly in his dream, pawing the ground. Sweat was loosening the dried caked blood on my face. I didn't like the taste of it. "You'll have to be quiet," I told them. "The stableboy next door might hear you."

Jay Jay prodded my hurting kidney with his iron. "That's his problem. Let's go."

As I stepped inside the dark stall, a shaft of moonlight picked out a huddled form in the corner. I walked the other way toward the inside partition. Charnock and Jay Jay were at my heels. I saw a dark shape near the wall, eyes looking down at me. There was a half-railing between us.

"Willie left it in his saddlebag. Down on the floor."

Charnock pushed me aside. "Where? I don't see anything."

"Too dark," I whispered. "Strike a match."

The match scratched and sputtered. A loud whinny from the dark stall caused Charnock to start nervously, drop the match. He struck and lit another. As he stooped forward, the restless moving shadow inside neighed, whistled through its nostrils. It reared high over us. Jay Jay and Charnock looked up startled as the black shape struck savagely at the rail. The thin boards splintered, fell away, and I had a chance.

"What the hell—?" Charnock said angrily. He looked up as Sister Sally, whistling shrilly, burst through like a dark avenging fury. She struck at Charnock, her hooves flailing. He screamed and went down. I chopped the gun out of Jay Jay's hand. He stopped to look for it and I tagged him with a long right. He staggered back and I went after him, remembering how badly he'd hurt me. Charnock was still down, trying to crawl away.

I saw Joey Zale on his feet holding a shotgun. "Hold it!" I yelled and hit Jay Jay a few more times. He got up and I kicked him viciously in the groin. He fell forward and I drove my knee up through his teeth. I had an idea Jay Jay might have held Willie's head under water for Charnock and I enjoyed what I was doing to him.

Jay Jay went down gurgling and stayed there. I heard heavy crunching sounds and turned. Sister Sally was over

Charnock going up and coming down hard. She was making up for all the years she hadn't been a winner.

She did front kick (*mae-geri*) and side kick (*yoko-geri*) and then added back kick (*ushiro-geri*) as she whirled and stomped and snorted. She did it with both feet very effectively. I never before had realized that horses knew karate.

Joey Zale was yelling, tugging at my arm. "Roper, for Christ's sake, what the hell is going on?"

I looked down at where Charnock was as the nervous mare came down on him again. "He was looking for Willie's diary," I said.

"I thought you already had it," Zale said. "Anyway, you shoulda warned the guy. You know how excited Sister Sally gets when somebody lights a match near her."

Twenty-eight

Early Saturday morning I drove down to the EPT office. I was still punchy after the hammering I had absorbed the night before. I figured I could heal just as well at my desk, looking at the mail, checking the duty roster. I owed O. J. a week's time.

The office was empty except for a blonde, sitting at my desk. She was young, fresh-looking, pretty, had all her own teeth, her marbles, and a lot more I could see through my puffed half-open eyes.

"Are you Mr. Roper?" she asked. I nodded dumbly, and she smiled and handed me a small folded piece of paper.

I read the scrawl on the missing last page of Hunter's diary. *Roper, this will introduce Pam Clayton. She's flipped lately. Got the idea I'm going to get killed, plus a lot of other things she says will happen, too corny to mention. Talk to her and try to straighten her out. Your old pal, Willie.*

I goggled stupidly at the page. There weren't any last-minute revelations. If Hunter knew who was killing him, he still hadn't put it down. It's not always that simple. You never know when you've already had your last drink, your last day. You think you're going to get up and have another crack at it, do it right this time, only you don't get the chance.

The girl sat quietly watching me stare and headshake it all out of my system. "What the hell are you doing here?" I barked finally. "I've been looking for you all over hell-and-gone."

She shrugged. Even with half-vision I could tell she had nice shapely shoulders. "Willie told me to come here and wait for you. That your office was the safest place for me."

"You've been here all the time?"

"Every day. You don't get many phone calls."

I looked down sourly at this bit of fluff who had worried the hell out of me. I wondered how the hell you went about spanking an heiress who probably had fifty-some-odd millions. "Okay," I said. "I found you. You're no longer a missing person. Now what do we do?"

She glanced at her watch. "They're running the Junior Miss Stakes today at Del Mar. It's for two-year-olds and fillies."

I remembered she had her own horse. "Are you running Mary Jane?"

"I would," she said slowly, "if I could borrow six hundred dollars from somebody. Daddy cut off my allowance."

I took out my roll, squinted the good eye at it. It sure is hell to be rich.

"Come on," I told her. "Maybe we can work it out."

She got up and came over. All her moving parts moved well. "Work what out?"

"My reward," I said.

She glanced at her watch again. "Well," she said. "Post time isn't until two o'clock."

About the Author

KIN PLATT was the newspaper cartoonist of the comic strip *Mr. and Mrs.* for the New York Herald Tribune Syndicate. His theatrical caricatures have also been featured in many newspapers and magazines. He is currently living in Los Angeles. He has written several popular juveniles, among them *Sinbad and Me*, which won the Edgar Award from the Mystery Writers of America for the best juvenile mystery of the year. He has written three previous adult mysteries: the first two, *The Pushbutton Butterfly* and *The Kissing Gourami*, feature private eye Max Roper; in the third, *Dead As They Come*, there is Molly Mellinger, New York mystery editor and amateur detective.